The Bridge Between Worlds

The Bridge Between Worlds

by

Stephen M. DeBock

Gypsy Shadow Publishing

The Bridge Between Worlds

by

Stephen M. DeBock

Gypsy Shadow Publishing

Lockhart, TX

www.gypsyshadow.com

Library of Congress Control Number: 201

eBook ISBN: 978-1-61950-040-2
Print ISBN: 978-1-61950-227-7

Published in the United States of America

First eBook Edition: Nov. 30, 2014
First Print Edition: June 23, 2014

For Ron Lindquist, David Ballentine, and Dale
Zelko: ERB-ophiles all

There's a hell of a good universe next door;
let's go.

—e. e. cummings

Prologue

From the Baltimore *Sun*:

REPORTER KILLED IN SKYDIVING ACCIDENT

SALISBURY, MD—A skydiving mishap has cost the life of a well-known feature writer for this newspaper. Lynda Murray, 26, perished when her parachute failed to open. She was a veteran of over 100 jumps.

Murray was the correspondent who penned the popular "Girls Do It" feature that appeared monthly in Sunday's edition of this newspaper. The column chronicled her forays into offbeat and occasionally dangerous hobbies and pursuits, especially those favored mostly by men. Last September, she learned of a parachuting school located at Walker Field, here, and signed up for a jump course. She wrote a full-page article about her experience, complete with freefall photographs, in a subsequent "Girls Do It" column.

Having become enamored of the sport, Murray coupled her love of skydiving with her growing affection for the airport's owner, Mr. Alden Walker. The two were married last Saturday while enroute to jump altitude in the center's airplane. Their plan was to be pronounced man and wife during freefall by the Rev. Donald Wilson, a fellow parachutist. They were then to perform aerial maneuvers for the entertainment of their guests on the ground before opening their chutes.

Features editor George Murray (no relation), an invited guest, reports that whereas the parachutes of Walker and the minister deployed normally, "Lynda's never came out of her pack. All of us could see her struggle to pull the ripcord. When she finally pulled her reserve, it was just too late." He added, "Lynda was a vital part of our *Sun* family. She will truly be missed."

Murray's parents are deceased and she had no siblings. She is survived by her husband, Alden James Walker. The Hemby Funeral Home, Salisbury, is in charge of arrangements. Rev. Wilson, acting as spokesman, has asked that in lieu of flowers, memorial gifts be made to the donors' favorite charities in the name of Lynda Murray Walker.

Chapter 1

I could tell Gus wanted to smack me—hard—upside the head.

"When are you gonna stop moping around, Numbnuts? Two months and you still won't get back on the horse that throwed you. Fly a plane. Take a jump. Even better, take a student pilot up, run a jump lesson, earn the company some money for a change."

I attempted to deflect the sting with a weak stab at humor. "Just so I'm clear on this, Gunny. You're calling the man who signs your paychecks *Numbnuts?*"

He tried to look contrite, something he was never able to do. "Oh, I'm sorry; *Mister* Numbnuts—*sir*." He scowled and shook his head, his short gray hair still cut high and tight and flat on top, just as it had been when he was in the Marines. "Come on, Walker, all due respect to Lynda, you're not the one screwed up. I've told you every day, every way I know, and you know I'm right. From now on, convince yourself. And do it fast." He put his hands on his hips, as he used to do when he wanted to intimidate recruits. "I'm carrying your load as well as mine around here, and my sea bag's gettin' kinda heavy. Know what I mean?"

I had to admit he was right. I was as useless as teats on a boar hog since what folks euphemistically called *the accident.* Don Wilson, Nate the jump pilot, Lisa the head instructor, Dennis the chief rigger, all the club members—they knew full well accidents are caused; they don't just happen. And they were kind enough never to mention the obvious—that I was made a widower after forty-five seconds of married life because of human error, not mechanical. And the human in question wasn't me.

So here I stood, in the ops building next to the airport parking lot and directly across from the jump school, attempting the impossible: staring down my former drill instructor, now my fixed-base operation's chief administrator. Gus ran the FBO with the same no-nonsense, by-the-numbers approach he'd used on the grinder at Parris Island. And his calling me *Numbnuts* was mellow. I can remember from when I was an eighteen-year-old recruit his getting within two inches of my nose, his stogie breath nearly gagging me, screaming all sorts of imprecations and aspersions upon my ancestry. I remember too, his famous threat to the platoon, which he regularly made good on to individuals throughout our boot training: "You little pissant, I've decided I'm *not* going to chew your ass out! No, private! I'm going to chew *around* your ass, and let it fall out by *itself!*"

From day one, when my ragged platoon mates and I had to stand on the painted yellow footprints in our first formation, eyes front, thumbs on our trouser seams, heels together, feet at a forty-five-degree angle, Staff Sergeant Bellows (how appropriate the name) and his two junior drill instructors rode us hard, kept reminding us that we weren't Marines, we wouldn't make a pimple on a Marine's ass, we were nothing but a bunch of high school pussies. And they kept reminding us there were: "only two ways to get off my beloved Parris Island—in a Marine Corps uniform or in a pine box." Most of the recruits both feared and hated their DI's. But I didn't. Well, I admit to a certain amount of fear. But I had gone in knowing what they had to do.

First they broke us down. Then they built us up. And twelve weeks from the day we had stood as civilians on those yellow footprints, we graduated as Marines, our rifle marksmanship badges pinned proudly to our greens. I had PFC chevrons on my sleeves as well.

Next time I saw Bellows was a couple of years later at Marine Barracks, Washington, D.C. He was a gunnery sergeant by then, finishing out his career doing ceremonial duty—as platoon sergeant to my right guide. I jumped when the lieutenant introduced him to the platoon, and he remembered me and laughed. The rest of the platoon did, too; they knew that only one thing could make any Marine jump—the unexpected sight of his old DI.

Turned out we got along fine, and we both received our discharge papers on the same day. We spent the night before in the slopchute, buying beers for the guys, then spent the next morning recovering from vicious hangovers, crawling into our civvies, and checking out for the last time.

We were discharged on a Friday, and that night we attended the weekly Moonlight Parade we'd marched in for two years but had never seen from the stands, among the thousands of civilian attendees. The troops—the guys we'd been drinking with the night before—did just fine without us. Isn't that the way? No one is indispensible.

As a new civilian, I spent my days as a nine-to-fiver, my nights in a community college, and weekends pursuing a newfound passion at a Maryland flight training school. Then my parents died, and their farm on the DelMarVa Peninsula became mine.

I hated farming.

But I loved flying. It's what kept me going on the weekends when I was a cubicle clone. So I cleared off their land, rustled up some backers, and found the best person possible to help me wade through the FAA's quagmire of paperwork. That person was Gunnery Sergeant August Bellows, USMC, retired.

They say you can make a small fortune owning an airport—if you start with a large one. I spent most of my own money and a whole lot more of the bank's before Walker Field finally became operational. After we had managed to stay a step or two ahead of the bill collectors, I added some ratings to my pilot's license and started training students, while Gus marched right into the managerial role he was born for.

Then one day he asked me, "You ever try skydiving?"

Chapter 2

Ten delicate fingers covered my eyes from behind. "Guess who, Alden?"

It could only be—

"Jennifer Bellows."

"Right!" she squealed, spun me around, and hugged me. Tight. The girl had more boobs than brains, but I didn't dare even think that, not with her uncle in the office, glowering at her as only he could. Glowering, but as protective of her as a mother grizzly is of her cubs.

"My shitbird brother," announced Gus, "took his airhead trophy wife—number three or four, I've already lost count—and headed to their Eye-talian *vee-la* for the summer. So guess who gets to watch the twerp here while they're gone—again."

"It's the fourth wife, Unca Gus, and you know that." She added a mock curtsy. "And as you know, I am the product of Number One." She looked pointedly at me. "As in, Oops. Daddy made sure he never made *that* mistake again." She held up two fingers, as if they were scissors. "Snip, snip."

Gus was still scowling. Which, by the way, looked a lot like his smile. Sometimes it was hard to tell if he liked you or loathed you. Until he said something, that is; if he chewed you out, he liked you. It meant you were worth his attention.

I said, "So, for the record, why aren't you spending the summer with Wife Number One? Just curious. Not that we don't want you here, understand."

"Number One's singing with the angels," she said, which brought me up short. "I never knew her. Two and Three support themselves with alimony and, who knows, sugar daddies maybe. Oh, by the way, Unca Gus, I'm not a twerp anymore. I'm eighteen now. Legally an adult. I can like help out and everything."

"So like grab a broom, and like make yourself like useful."

"A broom? Puh-lease."

"So, Jennifer," I said. "You heading to college in the fall?"

Gus rolled his eyes up. "I can answer that. She's still sucking at the family teat."

Jennifer ignored him. "Not just yet, Alden." Her expression became pseudo-philosophical. "I figured I'd take some time off to, like, find myself, you know?"

"Find yourself? I didn't know you were lost."

She slapped me on the arm. "Come on, you know what I mean. I mean, look around you." She made a sweeping gesture. "The airport. The jump school. You found yourself."

Gus chuckled. "Walker found himself at twelve, and he's been playing with himself ever since."

"Unca Gus!" she said, trying to contain a laugh. "That's not nice!"

I added, "And how would you know, Gunny? You didn't meet me 'til I was eighteen. Maybe you're talking about yourself and not me."

"It's universal," he said. "Been going on since Christ was a corporal."

"Stop it, you two, right now. You're making me blush."

"That'll be the day, Blondie."

Jennifer switched gears. "So, Alden, what are you up to these days?"

Great. As if I were in the mood for small talk. "Oh, saving third world countries, inventing new vaccines, rescuing damsels in distress; you know, the usual." I hadn't seen Jennifer since last summer, but she had to know about Lynda. Gus would've told her. I might have expected some expression of condolence at least. Or was it really just all about her?

"Walker here is heading to the USPA championships in Arizona," Gus said. News to me, but I tried not to show surprise; he was up to something, and from Parris Island on I'd learned to trust him. When I saw Jennifer's crestfallen look, I realized what it was. "Leavin' in a day or two. Yep. Gone for at least a week, maybe two . . . maybe more."

Thanks, Gunny.

Jennifer looked at me with sad blue eyes. "Really, Alden?"

I nodded, trying to appear apologetic.

"He's takin' that Skylane sittin' outside on the ramp," Gus added. "Needs a good shakedown cruise, and he hasn't had time to give her one yet."

"Is it new?"

"New to us."

"Oh." A pause. "Can I go?"

"What!" Had Gus still been a smoker, he would've swallowed his stogie.

"Unca Gus, I am an adult now."

"You're also an idiot if you think I'm—"

"Wait a minute," I interrupted. "There's no way you're going with me, Jennifer . . . much as I'd love to have you." I shot a glance at Gus. "But I need the time to myself right now. You understand." It wasn't a question, and she finally got the message.

"Oh. Yeah, guess I do. Sorry about your loss." Her mouth twisted, and she muttered to herself, "Looks like I'm going to have another whoop-de-do summer."

The gunny had saved my bacon, twice with one blow: forcing me back into the air to: a) snap me out of my funk; and, b) escape the clutches of his crush-prone niece. I'd never be able to thank him enough. And he'd never let me forget it.

By next afternoon, the Cessna was gassed up and packed with my duffel, jump suit, and parachute pack. Jennifer and Gus saw me to the plane, and she gave me another boobalicious hug before I climbed aboard. If I were eighteen again . . . no, don't even go

9

there. She was beautiful, sure, and no doubt willing—hell, downright horny—but Lynda was still very much on my mind.

Besides, her uncle still had his standard Marine Corps issue .45-caliber Colt, and he knew how to use it.

Chapter 3

Jennifer Bellows followed her uncle into the operations building and looked out the window as the blue and white Cessna Skylane, registration number N6124Q, fired up its engine. She listened for the engine runup, saw Alden in the left seat wiggle the ailerons, work the rudder and elevator, then pick up the mic and look at the building as he transmitted his message:

"Ops, Cessna Two Four Quebec, radio check."

Gus, standing at the desk, picked up his microphone. "Two Four Quebec, loud and clear. Now get out of here."

The second radio in the building was tuned to the flight service station frequency. They listened as Alden Walker activated his instrument flight plan.

"Why's he filing instruments, Unc? It's clear as a bell up there."

"Shouldn't have to remind you, twerp, Walker's a belt and suspenders guy. But look again. It's only clear straight up. Look out ahead and you can see the schmutz."

"Oh, right, an inversion. Cold air sits on top of the hot. Makes haze. See? I remember from last year."

"Okay then, Amelia Earhart. What does an inversion do to forward visibility?"

She smiled. "It makes it suck."

"Will you stop using that expression?"

Jennifer leaned across the desk and shook her head. Her long blond mane flew about her face. It was an unconscious affectation. "I thought if I like, knew something about flying, Alden . . . Do you think he likes me, Unca Gus?"

"What—Walker? Don't be an idiot. He's ten years older than you are. And hello? May I remind you that he just lost his wife?"

"Well, I'm sorry about that. But hello yourself, isn't it about time he moved on?"

Gus shook his head as he sat at the desk and pulled out some paperwork. "I am so glad I never had kids."

"None that you know about, Unc." She winked; he scowled.

Jennifer walked out to the drop zone to watch the last brace of parachutists for the day float to the earth. *Not for me,* she thought. *Why anyone would want to jump out of a perfectly good airplane is beyond me.* She strolled the apron past the flight school's single-engine airplanes and continued down the ramp where the privately owned planes were tied down. Most were low-wing Pipers or high-wing Cessnas. She patted the cowling of a sleek-looking Mooney she hadn't seen before and looked inside the window. *All those tiny little round gauges,* she thought, *how does anyone keep an eye on all of them? How can anyone remember what they all mean?*

An old, school-bus-yellow Yankee danced off the runway—a two-seater, it had half the number of seats as Alden's Cessna. Jennifer glanced at her watch. *I'm getting hungry,* she said to herself as her stomach growled. *Chinese tonight? God, I hope Unc doesn't make SOS for breakfast tomorrow.*

The Yankee made a couple of touch and goes before taxiing back to its tiedown. The pilot, an overweight old man with a white goatee that made him look like the face on a KFC tub, did his postflight inspection—he stroked his plane like a lover; *hello, it's a machine, dipwad*—and walked toward his car, whistling. The jump plane was back on the ground and being secured for the day. The airport grew still.

Then Jennifer looked up and saw an airplane approach, silhouetted against the lowering sun. From the overhead wing, she knew it was a Cessna. As it drew closer, she saw it was blue and white. And as it entered the traffic pattern, she was able to read the N number on its fuselage. She ran into the office.

"Unca Gus, Alden's back. Think he changed his mind about taking me with him?"

They stood outside the building and watched the plane land. Gus frowned. "Probably something wrong with it. Like I said, Walker never got the chance to give it a shakedown."

The plane taxied to the ramp and the propeller stopped. Gus scratched his head. "Did you hear that?" he asked.

"Hear what?"

"Nothing. Literally. The engine. It didn't make a sound. Engines make sound."

The plane's door opened, and the pilot got out. He looked like the proverbial cat that had swallowed the canary.

Gus could only stare. Jennifer began to tremble as the color drained from her face.

The pilot was definitely Alden Walker. But he was also definitely not Alden Walker. He was wearing his yellow jumpsuit, which he hadn't had on when he'd left. And it was patched in places, wrinkled, totally un-squared away, totally unlike Alden. His physique was different, too: leaner, but somehow more muscular; his jump suit stretched tight across his chest; and there was something about his nose . . . He wasn't wearing his wedding ring, either. But the most amazing thing was none of the above.

In the two, maybe three, hours since he'd been away, Alden Walker had grown a month's worth of beard.

Chapter 4

Obviously, I'd had no intention of going to Arizona. First, I'd never been a competitive skydiver and didn't intend to start now; second, the Nationals weren't until the fall anyway. But Jennifer didn't know that. I had filed my flight plan for a small airport I liked near the foothills of Virginia's Blue Ridge Mountains, confident that if Jennifer had been listening to my transmission in the office and questioned it, Gus would tell her Virginia was my first overnight. Flying at a speed of around one-fifty, you don't make Arizona in a single day.

What I'd do and where I'd go next, I had no idea. I'd kept in touch with some Marine Corps buddies scattered up and down the East coast, and maybe I could make a round robin out of this. However, I knew I couldn't stretch the trip out more than a couple of weeks, which meant I'd have to come back and face Jennifer eventually. But there'd be a lot of work to catch up on, and I'd be conveniently busy. For a while, anyway.

Not that I was afraid of Jennifer, mind you (although her uncle could still give me pause), and I had no illusions about my irresistibility to the opposite sex. I kind of felt sorry for her, being sloughed off to her uncle these two summers while her father and her latest stepmother vacationed in Tuscany or wherever. Maybe that was part of the reason she was so clingy. I appreciated that, truly I did. But last year, when this whole summer visitation thing started, Jennifer built me up in her mind to be something more than I am and established her reputation as—well, as a pest.

Miss Velcro. She returned to her father's tony George-town address over Labor Day weekend, and Lynda walked into my life seven days later.

The haze at four thousand feet was almost impenetrable. Visibility down was okay, but straight ahead I had maybe four miles—legally visual flight conditions, but if one of those jets from Pax River Naval Air Station suddenly appeared in your windshield practicing low-level maneuvers at three hundred knots, you wouldn't even have time to release your bowels before you and the other guy blew up. Filing instruments and having your flight monitored by Air Traffic Control was the best insurance policy you could buy. And it was free, courtesy of our rich uncle—you know, Sam.

A look up through the Plexiglas windshield revealed a bright blue sky. I keyed the mic and asked Air Traffic Control for permission to climb. That's the negative part of instrument flight: you have to ask permission from ATC just to pick your nose. Using visual flight rules, you can pretty much climb or descend at will. If you see something interesting below, you can circle it a few times, maybe even take some pictures, and not worry about sending someone on the ground, watching your transponder code on a radar screen, into a hissy fit.

"Two Four Quebec, climb to six thousand approved. Notify at altitude."

"Two Four Quebec." I added power and began climbing, watching the blue above me grow brighter, and before long I broke out with five hundred feet to spare. Here the air was severe clear, with no turbulence, and the cockpit climate went from muggy to mild. A minute or so later I leveled out. "Center, Two Four Quebec reporting six thousand."

The controller acknowledged, and I slid the seat back a little on its tracks to enjoy the ride. At times like this, with the nearest human beings more than a mile away straight down, I thought back to my Marine Corps days and remembered some of the more—um, ribald ditties we used to sing: "Roll Your Leg Over,"

"Barnacle Bill the Sailor," and "Roll Me Over in the Clover" came to mind, plus the myriad limericks set to music, beginning with "There once was a man from Nantucket." A far, far cry from the poetry I enjoyed in my college lit classes. But my favorite among them was one that was a little more creative and a lot less filthy, and I figured why not belt it out, there's no one around to hear me:

"Here is to Eve, the mother of our races.
She wore fig leaves in the right places.
Here is to Adam, the father of us all.
For he was Johnny on the spot when the leaves began to fall."

My thoughts drifted to happier days. Flying put me literally above my earthly cares and woes, and I found myself smiling for the first time since . . . well, since. I continued:

"Mary had a little watch, she swallowed it one day.
Her mother gave her castor oil to pass the time away.
The castor oil, it did not work, the time it did not pass,
So if you want to know the time, just look up Mary's—"

"Two Four Quebec, Center, descend and maintain four thousand."

This was unexpected. Four grand would put me back in the soup. It was beautiful up here, and I could even see the Blue Ridge Mountains way ahead. In fact, the weather had improved dramatically. Through the windshield I could spot the checkerboard farmlands leading up to the mountains. In a matter of minutes, I'd have the airport environment in sight.

"Center, Two Four Quebec will proceed in accordance with visual flight rules and add five hundred feet to altitude. Please cancel IFR flight plan."

"Roger, Two Four Quebec. IFR terminated. Have a good day, sir."

I clicked the mic switch twice and looked between the seats for my flight bag, where I kept my sectional charts. I unzipped the bag, reached inside, found the well-worn folded paper, and took it out. That was all the time it took before I looked back up and saw another Cessna nearly filling my windshield, heading straight at me.

Chapter 5

On instinct, I yanked the yoke hard right just as the other pilot banked to his right. We veered off, missing each other by what must have been fifty yards, but seemed like inches. I'd always thought the expression "My heart was in my throat" to be a bit overdone. Believe me, it's not. I had to gulp hard, over and over, just to swallow it back down.

Again on instinct, I straightened the wings and returned to level flight. I turned in my seat to look out the Skylane's rear window at the other plane. My hands trembled, my heart fluttered, and my sphincter struggled to unpucker. Outraged, I watched the other plane tilt from side to side, wagging its wings in the traditional pilot's salute. "I've got your salute!" I shouted, making a fist and extending my longest finger skyward. "Right here!" Then I turned back to face front—and panicked all over again.

There was a hole in the air. Sounds ridiculous, but that's what it was. A hole. Huge. Right in front of me. And close. So close there was no way to go around it, or above it, or below it. You can't put on the brakes and back up in an airplane.

I remember thinking: How could there be a hole in the air?

In that split second before I flew through, I got my last glimpse of the Virginia piedmont. Then, suddenly, I was looking down, wa—a—ay down, at desert scrub. The distant Blue Ridge Mountains were gone. In their place a plateau rose straight up from the desert, with other mountains even farther away, jagged purple teeth reaching up to snag a few passing clouds.

I looked behind me. Through the rear window I saw the hole close like the iris of a camera, its blurry edges coming together to obliterate the world I knew, and when it closed completely it was as if nothing had been there at all but sky. Blue sky. Like mine, but not mine.

First rule in an emergency: fly the plane. I took several deep breaths, flexed my feet on the rudder pedals, wiggled my damp fingers on the yoke, and checked my instruments, none of which thought anything was wrong.

Second rule: announce. I keyed the mic and called center. No response. I dialed the emergency frequency, 121.5. Guaranteed, someone would hear me. "Any aircraft or flight service station, this is Cessna Six One Two Four Quebec, declaring emergency."

Nothing.

I called again. And waited. Some static would be nice, I thought, but I couldn't even get that, except when I turned the Squelch button hard right. I turned it back and tried yet again. "Cessna Two Four Quebec, mayday. Repeat, Two Four Quebec, mayday." I was in some sort of radio Death Valley. I hung up the mic and tossed off my headphones, but all I could hear now was the engine noise. I patted the glareshield and said, "We're not in Kansas anymore, Toto."

Two Four Quebec reached the plateau, and we were now only about a thousand feet above ground level. Below me lay grassy fields, stands of forest, and in the distance those mountains, now closer. One was cone-shaped and snow-capped, looking like an extinct volcano.

And speaking of volcanoes, lava began gurgling in my stomach. Before long it had spread to my small intestine. If it reached the large one, I'd soon be in deep . . . trouble. Logic told me that since I didn't know where I was or where I was going, it might be wise to find a level stretch of ground to land on and try to get my bearings. Most of the land here was relatively flat, and the meadow grass didn't seem too tall. I set up an approach, eyeballing my altitude, and lowered the Skylane easily onto the ground. My landing roll was short and relatively smooth, considering the grass hadn't been groomed for me.

By now it was getting tough to breathe, and I flipped open the side window to gulp in some sweet air before pulling back on the fuel mixture knob and shutting down the engine. I turned off the key and listened to the gyros wind down, sucking in deep breaths all the while.

They didn't help. I opened the door and fairly leaped from the plane, fumbling with my belt as I tried to get some real estate between the Skylane and me before losing it, literally.

I won't describe the next few minutes, except to say the pause that refreshes really didn't. My face felt flushed, I could barely stand, and a troop of Boy Scouts was using my intestines for knot-tying practice. Leaving the unfortunate bush behind, I staggered back to the plane and sat in the shade of the wing. I wondered if I looked as bad as I felt, but decided I didn't want to know.

The sun began to set in the west, and as the sky darkened a full moon rose in the east.

I hurt, and I was tired, and I wanted to go to sleep. With my mouth gulping in air like some slack-jawed idiot, I watched the moon's progress above the horizon. Big and orange it was, a familiar tie to something comfortingly prosaic. Except for one tiny detail that threw me into yet another panic attack.

The man in the moon was missing.

Chapter 6

The mountain that looked like an inactive volcano was exactly that—and in an earlier age had been excavated to provide comfortable living and working accommodations for scores of people. Inside a large room filled with a vast array of technology, a young woman and her father stood before a viewscreen that nearly filled one wall. They were watching a small airship, with its operator propped against a landing gear leg, unmoving, perhaps unconscious.

"It worked," said the man, unnecessarily. He was the senior member of this community, whom some addressed as Patriarch.

"But at what cost, old man? We do not have enough Power left to send him back."

"Which gives him a strong reason for completing his task, does it not?"

The woman shook her head. "I wish we had not done this. It is not fair to conscript an offworlder to do our fighting for us. I wish you had simply let me and a team of—"

"It would be suicide," he admonished her. "They would be aware of your coming and easily kill you all. Which means not one but two of the people I love most would be taken from me. And we would be no better off for your sacrifice."

"But they have already taken two of the three people I love most, and I cannot bear to wait for someone else, someone who has no motivation other than self-preservation, to do what we should be doing ourselves. Our *champion,* lying there helpless, could be the rankest coward who ever walked on two legs. What then?"

"We have discussed this already." They had, in fact, more times than either cared to recount. "Remember, there is enough Power in the others' hands at this moment to threaten his own world, too. Better—"

"—that we risk one person now than all our people later. I know, I know." She was clearly tired of hearing the same arguments. They had become a litany by now. "So," she said, "while we stand here philosophizing, our unsuspecting hero lies next to his airship, probably sick unto death. I take it you will span him here directly for the antidote." Which begged the question, What are you waiting for?

"Immediately. If we lose him, his airship is useless to us."

"Father—never mind." She had accepted the reality, but she couldn't be so callous as her father seemed. Or was he just being practical?

The man activated a power switch on the console before him. "Go to the medical suite; I shall span him there."

"May I suggest you deliver him outside the mountain? Perhaps a hand's breadth above the ground? Remember, you have never spanned someone before; precision might be a problem."

"Understood." He turned to a series of controls that included a joystick and a slider mechanism and began to manipulate them as his eyes focused on the screen. The young woman studied the man as his image grew larger. She watched him twist and turn his body, obviously in distress, then saw him look up, with renewed fear, directly at where she knew the portal would be. Her father manipulated the controls, and the man disappeared.

"I shall fetch him," she said.

"Have An—have someone help you."

She looked at her father with hurt in her eyes. They had both suffered losses of late, and living with those vacancies, those holes, those canyons in their day-to-day existence sometimes seemed an insufferable challenge. "Galen will help me," the woman said with more tenderness than the simple statement warranted. Then she was gone.

Chapter 7

I prepared to die. I passed into and out of consciousness, and every time I came out my body was weaker and my pain was stronger. Maybe it was the pain that brought me back. All I knew was that I was in a world of hurt, and there was nothing I could do about it.

Looking up into the evening sky, I saw another hole like the one that brought me here, but smaller. What was going on? Airborne doughnut holes? Well, I wasn't going to fly through this one; that was for sure. Maybe if I held totally still . . .

But this time it was the hole that moved. Over me. Toward me. Around me. A sudden weightlessness overwhelmed me. Nausea came with it, but I'd already ralfed everything in my stomach, so all I could do was hurl blanks. It must've sounded wonderful.

I was floating . . . "What are you doing, Dave?" . . . "Help me, I'm melting" . . . "It was beauty killed the beast"—

—and my body thumped hard on the ground, near that cone-shaped mountain I'd seen earlier. A wooden building stood nearby, and something whinnied inside. A head looked out at me and whinnied again. A horse, I figured—then looked again, saw something that just couldn't be, and had to close my eyes.

A pair of arms struggled to lift me, and I heard a woman's voice. I couldn't understand her, but I managed to put my arm around her shoulders as she shuffled me into . . . somewhere. A few seconds later someone with a man's voice joined her to take my other arm. Words were exchanged, and the woman's tone suggested she was thanking the man for his help. As for me, I was just dead weight. But at least I wasn't dead. Yet.

How long I was out I couldn't say, but I remember being strapped to a gurney and having intravenous needles shoved into each arm. Within minutes the pain began to subside; either that, or I was being anesthetized. Someone put a sheath on me with a tube attached, so I could pee without wetting myself, and I felt relieved, no pun intended, that I'd taken care of that other function in the field. Something like a pair of buds was placed into my ears, and sounds came through that were gibberish at first, but eventually seemed to make sense. I drifted into and out of consciousness, and after what seemed a long, long while, I recognized some of the words the people tending to me had made; in fact, I understood them. I wasn't aware of having been transferred from the gurney to a bed, but on one of several trips back to consciousness I felt the softness of a mattress beneath me and the coolness of sheets around me.

Eventually the pain was gone, totally. My forehead didn't feel hot any more, and the needles were gone from my arms. My breathing was normal and deep. Nothing lodged inside my ears. I was asleep and would have been willing to stay that way for, say, a decade, but I sensed motion nearby, and then felt someone's hands pulling the sheet up from my waist to my shoulders. I realized I was naked under the sheet. A gentle hand brushed the hair back from my forehead and then stroked my cheek. Slowly, I opened my eyes.

Assuredly, I had died, and heaven—despite the sins of my youth—was mine. For this had to be an angel looking down at me, her face inches away and radiating compassion. What an exotic angel she was; unlike anything I'd ever seen before. Her skin was a cross between olive and copper, and her eyes were large, almond-shaped, and so dark brown as to be nearly black. Her nose was straight, with a tiny upturn at the tip, and her lips were wide and full. This exquisite face was framed by shag-cut black hair that on a mortal woman would look unkempt, but on her it looked brazenly beautiful.

She wore a white sleeveless top that flattered her figure and revealed some cleavage when she leaned forward. I admit it; men are pigs. But I did try to do the gentlemanly thing and keep my eyes on her face. One would not want to alienate an angel, after all.

Standing on the other side of my bed was an elderly man. His skin was the same color as the woman's, and his eyes were just as dark and vital. He wore a bushy beard, and his full head of hair was battleship gray, like Gus's, but not nearly so tightly trimmed.

"I bid you greeting," said the man as if he were a butler welcoming guests to a fancy dress ball. "Please do not be alarmed. My name is Oreste." He nodded toward the woman, which gave me license to look back at her. "My daughter, Sandrine."

I nodded to her. "Alden Walker," I managed to croak. My lips were as dry as the desert I'd flown over at some time in my recent past.

"Greetings to you, Aldenwalker," the lady said in a sweetly musical voice. When she said her next words, the music died. It wasn't so much the words themselves, it was the way she said them—tentatively, maybe even apologetically. "Welcome to Earth."

Chapter 8

Impossible. This wasn't Earth; this wasn't my Earth. My Earth, after all, had a view of the man in the moon. My Earth did not have what I'd seen in the stable after my body was unceremoniously dropped—teleported?—here. My Earth didn't even have teleportation. And it was peopled with friends like Gus, clinging vines like Jennifer, family like my late parents, a lover . . . Lynda.

Lynda, my bride of forty-five seconds: whose hair cascaded past her shoulders like a crimson waterfall; whose eyes were as green as a leprechaun's cap; whose nose was graced with the subtlest splash of freckles. Whose love was pure and unconditional.

A memory returned then, of when she'd accepted my proposal of marriage. I told her I loved her so much I'd gladly lay down my life for her. She laughed and said she would never die for me. "After all, mine is an undying love."

But she had died. And the next image to hit me was Gus' no-nonsense assertion that it was time to move on. I couldn't address that now, but in a real sense I had moved on. Rather, in some bizarre way I'd moved off . . . off my world and onto another.

As a kid I had devoured the Edgar Rice Burroughs novels, and my favorites had nothing to do with *Tarzan, Lord of the Jungle*. Instead, I was enthralled by his first efforts at science fiction, and in my adolescent fantasies I had pictured myself on Burroughs's Mars, a.k.a. Barsoom, with its attendant calots and thoats, and a green, four-armed friend named Tars Tarkas. Now, somehow, those fantasies were becoming real.

But I wasn't John Carter, *Warlord of Mars;* I was simply Alden Walker, citizen of Earth, transported somehow to an alternate Earth. Alter Earth? And staring at me was Alter Earth's equivalent of Dejah Thoris, the beautiful princess of Mars. But she was more beautiful than I'd imagined Dejah Thoris to be, and her name was—what?—Sandrine.

ERB's Martians were oviparous, I remembered. "Tell me," I mumbled weakly, "do you people lay eggs?"

She stood up straight and nearly laughed. "I assure you, Aldenwalker, that we do not. Why would you even think that? More to the point, why would that be the very first question out of your mouth?"

"Must be my delirium."

"No matter," said the man, also puzzled. "If you are feeling better, perhaps we can help you freshen yourself. And then tell you why I needed to span you from your world into ours."

My clothes had been cleaned, and after I dressed I joined Oreste and Sandrine outside my tiny room. In response to their question I told them yes, I was both hungry and thirsty, so off we went to the dining hall.

During my time as a Marine in D.C., I occasionally stood sentry duty in so-called *undisclosed locations* that were basically underground command posts carved into the landscape, to be used by the President in case of enemy attack. That said, it came as no great shock to learn I was now inside that conical mountain I'd noticed upon my sudden arrival here. The place looked industrially sterile, mostly grays and whites; but to its creators' credit, it didn't appear gloomy. Perhaps a hundred people of all ages populated this keep, as Oreste called it, and for reasons I'd soon learn, they rarely mingled with other people beyond it. When they did mingle, in fact, they religiously followed strict codes of confidentiality. Again, with my former top secret security clearance, this was not something I questioned. In fact, it was fine with me, as others' travels didn't interest me nearly so much as my own right about now.

The dining hall was about the size of the mess hall back in the Washington barracks, and at this time of day—sometime in mid-afternoon, I guessed—it was nearly deserted. The handful of people who were there sat in small groups and nodded politely in our direction as we entered. Their faces betrayed a variety of expressions as they looked at me, ranging from hopeful to hopeless. Hmm. What did they know that I didn't? All of them had that same olive-copper skin and dark hair. They dressed mostly alike, too—I got the impression of corporate casual Fridays—and the men all sported at least modest growths of facial hair. I felt my own stubbly face and longed for my Gillette.

Oreste fetched us an assortment of fruits and vegetables, bread, cheeses, and three mugs of a greenish tea sweetened with honey, and we sat down on three-legged chairs at an unoccupied circular table. We ate and sipped in silence for a few seconds, as if neither the man nor his daughter knew where to begin. So I did.

"Why did I get so sick?"

His answer was straight out of H. G. Wells, and it reminded me also of the non-fictional precautions taken with our returning astronauts during the Apollo program. "Native microbial contamination, for which your body was not prepared."

"And you were able to fix that?"

"Yes."

"Why can I understand you when you're not speaking English—and, by the way, neither am I?"

"While you were unconscious," said Sandrine, "you received subliminal linguistic instruction."

"And that's it?"

"That is it."

I grunted. "Thanks for sparing me the scientific details," I said. "They'd probably be Greek to me anyway."

Father and daughter exchanged glances. "Greek," she remarked.

"Ancient Hellas," he replied.

"I know that, old man," she said with some impatience.

"Children, let's not argue," I interrupted. "I've got a lot of questions yet."

"Apologies," said Oreste. "We were simply recalling our own history, when our ancient ancestors enjoyed much pleasant intercourse with the Hellenes of your world."

I almost coughed out a mouthful of tea. Me and my dirty mind.

Chapter 9

"There are nine known universes—or, perhaps, nine dimensions to our one universe," said Sandrine as I stuffed my face with bread and cheese, "but only two display similar evolutionary patterns. Technologically, our people evolved much more quickly than yours. In fact, our forbears developed the ability to bridge the worlds at the same time the Hellenes, or Greeks, if you prefer, of your world were just developing their democracy, literature, and art. A glorious time for them, we are told."

I'd have to admit this constituted much quicker progress, technologically speaking. But then, maybe this people had an earlier start than mine. Maybe they went directly from Australopithecus to Homo sapiens, without detouring through the Neanderthals, Cro-Magnons, and the multitude of others—a waste of hundreds of thousands of years, if you ask me. But you didn't ask me, and I digress. Oreste was speaking now.

"Liking the exotic sounds of the Hellenes' language, our ancestors took certain elements from it into our own. Names, for example. Mine means *From the mountain,* which is appropriate, considering that I was born here, and Sandrine's means *Saver of men.*" Suddenly he looked contrite, as if he had said something he shouldn't have.

"Not that I was able to live up to my name," she said bitterly. Her ebon eyes fixed on my baby blues: "What does your name mean, Aldenwalker?"

"I—uh, haven't the foggiest idea. Sorry. But what do you mean, you weren't able to live up to your name?" I asked.

"Later. Please . . . another time. The important thing is that our two ancient civilizations entered into certain exchanges of culture and tradition. What we liked, we kept. What they liked, they kept."

"Don't mean to interrupt," I interrupted, "but do I remember actually seeing a . . . a unicorn outside?" Sandrine said yes. "You know, they're mythical where I come from. I'm starting to see a connection here. How about centaurs? Minotaurs? Gorgons?" I was thinking of movies like *The Fly*, where human and insect molecules got mixed up in teleportation, producing somewhat less than lovely results.

The last word brought a sharp intake of breath from both of them. Sandrine gripped her mug so tightly I thought it might shatter. Oreste forced his expression blank.

"What do you know of gorgons?" he said.

"Well," I began, wondering what I'd said to upset them but happy to be on the instructing end for a change, "in Greek myth a gorgon is a woman with snakes for hair who turns everyone who looks at her into stone. In one story, a hero turns a gorgon named Medusa into stone by reflecting her image back at her in his polished shield. Close enough?"

"No."

"Oh."

He shook his head. "But we do have gorgons here. They are both female and male, but they have no connection to ophidians. They are . . . *ampairs*."

I got the translation instantly. "You're talking about bats, right? Little furry things? Live in the jungles, come out at night and drink cows' blood?"

"Hardly. These—"

"May we continue, old man?" I'd forgotten Sandrine for a second. Her father stopped, apparently happy for a reprieve. "Good," she said. "Aldenwalker, despite the similarities, there are profound differences between our two worlds. First, as we mentioned, we had evolved technologically eons before you. I am not being boastful, just factual."

"Go on."

"We had barely begun our lunar explorations when—"

"Stop, did you say lunar? As in, you had traveled to the moon? Thousands of years ago?"

"Yes. But certain . . . others were there, too. We worked peacefully and separately, mining the moon's surface, when we discovered—you understand that when I say *we* I am referring to our long-ago ancestors—we discovered a certain element, totally unknown here on Earth, possibly deposited by a meteor strike. It was ultra-light and ultra-reactive, and unlike any element we had ever classified. Due to its uniqueness, we came to call it simply the Power, and it had one salient property: it was inert—until it came into contact with gold. Then it detonated with horrendous force."

"No joke."

"I do not joke." She looked at her mug, empty now, and then at her father. "May we have more tea?"

I felt I could use some, too. Maybe the atmosphere was getting a little chilly. Oreste nodded and left us, mugs in hand.

"Forgive me if I appear brusque, Aldenwalker. What this leads to is very difficult for me. For both my father and for me. Doubly, perhaps, for me."

I tried to appear sympathetic, but my only real interest lay in how all this related to me.

Sandrine went on: "The Power was mined and brought to Earth."

"Why?"

"Because it could be harnessed. Every machine, from airships to timepieces, was eventually converted to run on the Power. A tiny handful could provide an entire city's needs for a score of lunes. And there was nothing generated from its combustion that would be detrimental to the environment. It was perfect."

"Wait a minute. If something sounds too good to be true, it is. Old Earth proverb."

Oreste brought us our refills and sat.

"You are correct," he said. "The flaw, though, was not found in the Power itself, but in the fact the others wanted it too, and whereas we were more than willing to share, they wanted it all for themselves."

"Let me guess. War."

"Total. After many conflicts, in which neither side emerged victorious, the others sent a missile to our lunar base—a missile with Power inside and tipped with a gold warhead."

Sandrine said, "Almost half the surface on that hemisphere of the moon was altered."

Oreste added, "Bits of the moon, hurled into space by the explosion, fell to Earth. Cities were destroyed, either from direct hits or from giant ocean waves. Seismic shocks lowered whole landscapes and raised others. All civilization, ours and theirs, was destroyed."

Sandrine sipped her tea and continued. "Those left alive had nothing. They did what was necessary to survive. But they were reduced to primitives. They had to begin their social and scientific evolution from the very beginning."

Oreste added, "And over countless generations, all knowledge of the Power was lost."

All right, but again, how did all this apply to me? Something was fishy with what they were telling me. I mean, obviously *someone* had knowledge of this Power. Oreste and Sandrine and those folks at the other tables, for starters. I'd save that question for later.

"I assume sometime between the discovery of this Power and the start of the all-out war is when you originally made contact with the ancient civilizations on my world?"

Oreste said, "Yes. Scientists discovered the parallel universes and a way to bridge them. Spanning required considerable amounts of Power, but at the time we had what we thought was an unlimited supply. However, early attempts in traversing the portal resulted in rather horrible deaths."

"Like mine would've been if you hadn't doctored me?"

"Yes. Science eventually found antidotes for the microbes, and successful exchanges were made between the universes—but then the war started and all contact was broken forever."

"Until now," Sandrine added.

"So. Did this . . . bridge . . . break down my atoms and transport them from my world to here, and then reassemble them? Is that how it works?"

"No," said Oreste with a chuckle, as if the idea were outrageous. "It merely opens a portal through which one can travel at will."

Or not at will. Hello? "So it's like opening a curtain and stepping through."

"Exactly."

"And if Mohammed doesn't come to the mountain, the mountain will come to Mohammed." As the portal had come to me when I lay dying by the plane.

Sorry, Scotty, you'll never get the chance to beam us up.

My thoughts went from futuristic sci-fi to the ancient Greek myths, of the gods on Olympus, of unicorns—which were real, I'd actually seen one in the stable outside—and drifted away from the history lesson. Not a good thing, because when my mind wandered back it heard Sandrine say, "You may not survive."

Chapter 10

In the aftermath of the War for Power, not everyone was reduced to savagery; random parts of the planet were spared from the cataclysm. These groups still had their machines, still had ample supplies of Power, and they decided to isolate themselves from those who might attack them for it, should they discover its existence. The hidden haves, the primitive have-nots. They formed their colonies far from populated areas and lived relatively comfortable lives while their counterparts began their long trek back toward civilization. They also structured a strict non-intervention policy; something thousands of years later on Alden Walker's Earth would take form in the mind of a science-fiction impresario named Gene Roddenberry, who dubbed it the Prime Directive.

One group was housed in a pre-war research station set up on a rocky plateau bordering the western ocean. A cliff rose from one side, and inside were working and living areas complete with all the comforts. A mountain spring provided water, and hydroponics provided vegetables for food. This was a small settlement, and the people's needs were simple. But inevitably, they grew lonely.

They began to scan for other sources of Power, and after much searching the settlers discovered another group like their own, but much larger, housed in a hollowed-out, long-dead volcano. Friendly contact was established and continued from generation to generation.

Midway between the two keeps, on the bank of a wide river, was a farming settlement that grew over time to become a substantial village. The inhabitants of the two keeps would often travel there in the guise of fellow villagers from far to the west and east. They adopted native dress, rode domesticated unicorns, and engaged in barter with the citizens of the village, which was named River's Reach.

It was not unusual for emotional attractions to form between members of the two different keeps. Less common would be bonds between the visitors and the villagers, but form some did. If they became strong enough for the pair to pledge, the townsman— or woman—would leave the village with his or her consort, to find a new home in the consort's keep. Thus did the hidden colonies grow and prosper—and maintain their secrecy.

With the passage of more than two millennia, all thought of the so-called others, the ones who had precipitated the War for Power, managed to devolve into the stuff of folk tales. It was to prove fatal.

Late one evening in present-day times, disaster struck at the seaside keep. Priam, his consort Ariadne, and their two young sons, had gathered around the communication screen linking them to the larger keep within the extinct volcano. The boys were eager to share the adventures of their day with the young couple and the older pair greeting them from so far away. Then, from the common room near to the main entrance, came a cacophony of roars and shouts, crashes and screams. Cries of *"Ampairs!"* filtered through the din, and the children stopped their chatter as their parents turned pale and searched frantically for a place for the family to hide.

It was too late. A large, brown, fur-clad form stood in the doorway—with long, muscular arms; with talon-tipped hands attached to the tops of translucent membranous wings; with drool spilling from its oversized jaws. It spoke but one word, and spittle sprayed from its mouth: "Blood."

Two more of its kind joined the first, whom they called Ibliss, and from whom they awaited orders. Priam and Ariadne held their sons tight, as if they could protect them. They had no weapon anywhere in their apartment; they had never had the need. The children whimpered in their parents' embrace, and their parents' blood turned cold when they heard the leader hiss, "You two, take the adults. The brats are mine; they're sweeter."

The gorgons leaped upon the huddled family and hurled them apart. Ariadne's head struck a table, mercifully knocking her unconscious. Priam was not so fortunate. He tried to fight his way to the children, but the gorgon who had selected him was too big and too strong. And too quick. His jaws snapped shut around Priam's neck, jerked once, and the man fell, his throat torn away. The gorgon dropped to his knees and buried his muzzle in Priam's neck as his counterpart slashed at the throat of Ariadne.

The leader, Ibliss, held the two screaming boys in his spidery fingers and hissed a sibilant laugh at the carnage before he took their lives, one at a time, as casually as one might swat a fly. When the three were finished gorging, Ibliss turned to go—and then stopped short. Something had caught his attention, something moving behind a screen built into the wall. He saw four horrified faces looking back at him. Even from behind the glass, he thought he could smell their fear. He drew back his lips, his dagger teeth dripping with gore.

One of the four made a quick move, and the glass suddenly went blank; but it was too late. Now the gorgon knew others were out there; others who also had the Power he had been seeking for so long, and he knew in time he would find them and take their Power, too, for his own.

There was no way Ibliss would have known or cared to know the names of those four whose shocked faces he had seen in the viewscreen. But the older pair were named Penelope and Oreste. The younger two were Ander and his consort Sandrine.

Chapter 11

Upon finishing the story, Sandrine lost her composure, her eyes filled up and spilled over. She turned to her father, and his dark eyes were damp, too. They lowered their heads and gripped each other's hands, and the few other people in the dining hall politely turned away.

Father and daughter took deep breaths. Embarrassment was evident in their expressions. "Damn," said Sandrine, wiping her eyes. "No napkins."

"I can get some," said Oreste, sounding anxious to be alone.

"Thank you, old man."

He stood, looked at me, and stopped. Sandrine noticed too. "We promised ourselves we would not let emotion take over," she said. "Now I see we have upset you as well."

I blinked and ran my fingers across my eyes. "Guess you did, at that. But I confess it wasn't for your story; it was for mine." I spoke the words that reopened the wounds. "See, I just lost my own wife—my consort—too. On the very day we exchanged our pledge."

Oreste moved behind me and placed a hand on my shoulder. Sandrine reached over and briefly touched my hand. "I am so sorry. We are linked in loss, Aldenwalker, all of us."

Her father walked to the serving counter and returned with cloth napkins. "Cotton," I observed.

"The keep works extensive farmland, on the far side of the mountain," he replied.

"We are self-sufficient," added Sandrine. "We lack for nothing."

If you lack for nothing, I thought, *then why did you need me here?*

And while I pondered that question, another part of me questioned the fairness of one group's having all the conveniences while the other, larger group—those in River's Reach and who knew how many other primitive settlements—had none of them; didn't even know about them, in fact.

But then there was the story of the goose who laid the golden eggs: If the farmer and his wife hadn't killed the goose but instead had kept it fat and happy; and had further shared their good news with their neighbors, well. It wouldn't have been long before the neighbors started demanding some of those golden eggs for themselves, and one of them would inevitably have killed the goose.

Plus, hadn't I read somewhere that more often than not big jackpot lottery winners ended up as bad as or worse off than they had been before? All things considered, *Star Trek*'s Prime Directive seemed eminently and ethically . . . logical.

Taking refuge in our own thoughts, we sat in silence. Finally, Sandrine brought us back. "The gorgons—probably a small raiding party—found us. It was easy. All they had to do was to fly east to the river and follow it past the village to our keep. Naturally, we were now posting guards every night, but on that night they were caught unaware and were overpowered before they could sound the alarm. Guarding the keep that night, as you have already surmised, were my mother . . . and my consort." She looked down again. "I was supposed to have joined Ander that night, but I was not feeling well, and my dear old lady took my place." Sandrine swallowed hard, self-recrimination in her tone.

Oreste asked, "Is it harder not to blame yourself when you are clearly not to blame? I too struggle with that."

I thought back to Lynda, our *wedding spectacular:* her idea; still, I faulted myself. After all, I could have said no. I should have said no.

Oreste looked at his daughter, who motioned that he be the one to go on. "The raid was carried out in silence. They came not for victims, but for Power. Six casks we had, enough to last centuries. When we woke the next morning, we found them gone, and at the guard post . . ."

Sandrine sat up straight, sniffing once. "We had only the Power left in our equipment reservoirs. And therein lay—lies—the problem."

"Why not just span your casks back? If you could bring me over, you could certainly . . ." They let me figure it out for myself. "Oh, yeah. Right. Yo-yo time. Then, why not—" I cut myself off; my mouth was working faster than my mind. "I give up. What?"

"Here we had a difference of opinion," said Oreste. "My daughter wanted to form an army, march on the seaside keep, destroy the gorgons, and take back the Power."

"I still feel that way."

"Yes. But the rest of us voted to do something a bit more prudent. Radical, I admit, but prudent. You see, it would take a long time to reach the gorgons' keep. Our little army could have been observed at any point on their journey, especially as the gorgons had learned to use the scanning device. And if they could be seen, they could be attacked. Further, we do not know how many gorgons are actually housed in the keep. We only saw three through the viewscreen, but we know there are more. Probably many more. Which means that even if our cadre made it to the keep, they could easily be overwhelmed."

"Right," I said. "You'd be better off with a swift team. In and out."

The two stared at me, eyeballs to eyeballs to eyeballs. Uh-oh, I was starting to get the old man's drift. And beginning to feel mighty uncomfortable.

"Swift team. Stealth operation. You needed me for that?"

Oreste said, "Not you, personally—how could we have known you even existed—but your airship. The plateau abutting the science station was in those times used by airships. But airships do not exist in our world anymore. I reasoned if we could span one from your world, along with someone to fly it, we— that is, one of us, along with the operator—could slip in during daylight, when the gorgons sleep. Together they could extract the Power and return it to the ship, then plant an explosive charge with a timed delay. Thus, we would regain the Power, and the gorgons would be obliterated."

"Ah, so let me see if I understand this. You don't really need *me*, you just need a plane and a warm body to drive it. Taxi service. You sent a scan into my world and plucked out the first plane you saw, and that happened to be mine. Hey, lucky me."

"Yes," Sandrine whispered. "And sarcasm does not become you."

"Thanks for that. So my job is to fly into a nest of *ampairs* to help you get your precious Power back." Another nod. "And what if I say no thanks, just send me back home?"

Oreste said, "Impossible. We have not enough Power remaining to send you back. You will need some of what is in those casks in order to return to your world."

"That was my objection," said Sandrine. "I have never believed in coercion, no matter the cause."

"I seem to remember your saying a while back that I might not survive."

"I did mention that, yes."

"Hmm. And who would this army of one be that I get to ferry to the keep? Whose chances, I'd guess, are about as gloomy as mine? Any volunteers?"

Sandrine glanced down at the table, then back at me. "We can discuss that later." She looked at her father, who ran his fingers angrily through his beard and left the table, scowling. When he was out of ear-shot, she said to me, "We have serious differences on that, but my mind is made up. One way or another, I am going to be that army."

Now I really felt plucked.

Chapter 12

I had never dreamed unicorns could be real, and now here I was, riding one. Well, just sitting on one, to be frank: a dun brown beast with its rein tethered to Sandrine's white mount in front of me. A man named Galen, a few years younger than I, rode a third—flanking me, probably to make sure I didn't fall off. His was a palomino-type gold, and both his and Sandrine's unicorns were at least a foot taller at the shoulder than mine. I felt like a kid at a county fair's pony ride. But hey, maybe that was a good thing. The only animal I'd ever ridden up 'til now was on a merry-go-round.

I had gone to sleep the night before in a pretty sour mood but woke up the next morning feeling a little better. Maybe part of it was the uniqueness: a world where bats had actually evolved alongside humans—and perhaps, thanks to the bridge, given birth to our own vampire mythos. Maybe another part was the Corps-fostered spirit of honor, country, and commitment, despite the fact this wasn't by any stretch my country, that my commitment was selfishly restricted to securing my return to my own world, discounting the fact I'd soon be facing some of the most fearsome suckers—literally—that ever lived.

Or maybe it was simply the fact that my task was unavoidable and I'd decided to make the best of it.

Then again, maybe Sandrine's smile of greeting that morning over breakfast had something to do with it. Think Barbie doll with a pixie cut. Or a life-sized Tinkerbell with black hair and olive-copper skin.

Widowed, like myself, and still loyal to the memory of her lost lover. In other words, colleagues; nothing more.

The dew still sparkled in the grass as we set out for the plane, which I was to fly back to the keep. Sandrine said she wanted to fly with me, and I was happy to oblige. As a flight instructor, one of my great joys has always been taking people up for their first flight in a small plane. Their invariable reaction after they've *slipped the surly bonds of earth* is invariably one of profound euphoria.

Then again, returning my thoughts to earth, maybe Sandrine was going along to make sure I didn't take off, do a one-eighty, and head for parts unknown.

An hour or so into our pseudo-horsey ride, I heard her voice drifting back and realized she was singing. There were no words to the song, just a slow, plaintive melody, with her mouth forming vowel sounds like a musical instrument. I remarked to myself that it was a far cry from the songs I'd sung in the plane, ditties whose vulgarity was a perfect match for my off-key croaking. Sandrine seemed oblivious to the two men behind her, or perhaps she was simply unselfconscious.

Galen said in a low and sympathetic voice, "Her consort wrote music. That is one of his compositions. Her favorite one."

"Oh."

Sunlight reflected off distant metal, and I knew we were close. Sandrine saw it too, stopped her singing, and spurred her mount to a trot, which unfortunately made my unicorn trot as well. I bounced in the saddle and figured my butt would be sore later. In fact, a neighboring area was already evidencing certain signs of distress more disturbing than that of my gluteus maximus.

We got to the plane none too soon for me, and once we had dismounted (I did this rather gingerly), Sandrine handed the reins to Galen. "I shall wait for you to become airborne before leaving for the keep," he said. Sandrine acknowledged him and began inspecting the plane, running her fingers over the white-painted aluminum, touching the rivets, feeling the decals that made up the blue accent striping, looking inside the cabin with what had to be wonder. This was something that hadn't been seen on Alter Earth for a couple of thousand years, and to her (Galen, too) it was a marvel to outmatch those even greater marvels in their keep, which they now no doubt took for granted.

I led Sandrine through the preflight inspection, from checking ailerons and flaps on the wings to the elevator and rudder at the tail. I lifted the inspection port, checked the oil level, and made sure no birds had made a nest inside the cowling. Next I opened the right-hand door and had my passenger sit inside. I showed her how to use the seat harness, closed her door, and climbed aboard through the pilot's door on the left side. I pulled, pushed, and turned the yoke, then worked the rudder pedals as Sandrine looked outside to see how they translated to the control surfaces. "Ready?" I asked, and she nodded enthusiastically.

I flipped open the side window, pushed the fuel mixture control in, opened cowl flaps, turned the master switch on, gave the primer a squirt, cracked the throttle a hair, shouted, "Clear prop" (from habit, Galen was nowhere near), and turned the ignition key. The propeller turned once, twice, and caught. Noise filled the cockpit, and it wasn't much diminished when I closed and locked the window. I didn't even think about it; two hundred thirty horses are bound to make some noise.

The unicorns probably made some noise, too; Galen was having a tough time controlling them.

I taxied back to where I'd landed originally, estimating I'd have plenty of room for the takeoff run. "How do you control our direction?" asked Sandrine, and I pointed to my feet. I pressed the right rudder pedal and we turned toward the right, then the left pedal to get us back on track. She nodded, taking in the gauges and controls and looking out the window as we got into position.

Engine runup came next. I applied the brakes (at the top of the rudder pedals, I pointed out), advanced the throttle, checked the operation of the magnetos, cycled the prop pitch, and reduced power again. I looked at the compass and set the directional gyro to match its reading, verified by the engine gauges that all was in order, set takeoff trim, looked at the glowing face of my passenger, and pushed the throttle forward.

Twenty degrees of flap added lift, and I pulled back on the yoke to get the nosewheel up as quickly as possible to reduce friction from the grass. Airspeed built up, and the Cessna grew lighter on the mains. When the wheels left the grass, I lowered the nose to level off and build some climb speed. Then with my fingertips, I eased the yoke back and Two Four Quebec pointed her nose at the sky.

A glance to my right showed that Sandrine was simply awed. Her head swiveled from window to windshield, turned toward the instruments and my left hand's delicate touch on the yoke as my right adjusted manifold pressure and RPMs. I almost expected her to say the people look like ants, but there were no people to see, Galen and the unicorns being far behind us now.

Before we left the keep, I'd picked out an appropriate landing spot, and as we approached the mountain I almost wished we could remain airborne longer. Flying is, for me, a supreme manifestation of fate control. It is ultimately my knowledge, my skill, and how I use both, that determine whether I live or die. Skydiving is much the same, although at this point I preferred not to think about that.

I told Sandrine to put the fingers of her left hand on the yoke on her side of the panel and rest her feet on the rudder pedals, and then let her fly the plane.

"Oh!" she cried as we porpoised through the air. "What am I doing wrong?"

"You're overcorrecting," I explained. "The controls are very sensitive. You have to train your fingers to the proper touch. Don't be discouraged; everyone over-controls at first."

"I like this!"

Soon, too soon, we had the landing area in sight. I had Sandrine continue to feather-touch the yoke as I brought the plane in for a reasonably smooth touch-down. Okay, we took a small bounce. But Sandrine didn't seem to mind; after all, what did she have to compare? I taxied near to the keep, braked, pulled back the throttle and then the mixture control. The engine died, the prop stopped, I turned the key, and the gyros whined as they wound down.

I turned to my passenger, who beamed like a kid at Christmas. Then her expression changed. She looked at me and said, in a voice suddenly business-like, "Aldenwalker, we have a problem."

Chapter 13

"This will not do," mumbled Oreste, his fingers fumbling through his beard. "This will not do at all."

The three of us stood alongside the plane, Sandrine trying to balance acknowledging the problem with her newfound glee at having defied gravity for the first time. A large group from the keep looked on from a respectful distance. I looked at Oreste, and if his language had a word for *duh*, I'd have used it. At him. "You know, airplanes do make noise."

"But the gorgons will hear you, even in the daytime." He shook his head. "No, this will not do at all. And yes, it was my oversight. Then again, my young friend," he said pointedly, "when we discussed what you call the *swift team stealth operation,* you might have mentioned your airship's penchant for noise."

Well, double-duh for me and a *touché* for him. I tried to look contrite. "You're right, old man, you're absolutely right. My bad."

Oreste looked uncomfortable, and Sandrine put a hand on his arm. "Aldenwalker, he is my old man, not yours. The term denotes a family connection—and family affection—and is used only by family members."

"So that's two gaffes I've made today, and it's not even lunchtime yet. No offense intended in either case, ol—Oreste."

"Indeed."

"You're supposed to say, 'None taken.'"

"Then, none taken."

Sandrine said, "To return to the matter at hand, we have a problem."

"No we do not," announced her father, as if a light bulb had just come on inside his head. "But we do have a delay." He turned to the crowd behind him and called out some names. Four men and two women came forward. "We need to make a silent engine for the airship," he told them. "One that is operated by the Power. Can we do it?"

One of them, a handsome woman somewhere in her mid-forties I'd guess, smiled confidently. "Of course we can. We can adapt the Powerplant from any number of our existing machines."

Here I hopped in. No way did I want my beloved Skylane dismantled, discombobulated, or in any other way cannibalized. "Wait a minute. That's not so easy as you might think. For one, the engine has to weigh the same as the one in there now. Otherwise, it'll throw off the—"

"Center of gravity," the woman said. "Weight and balance. We understand that."

I'd been put in my place, but there was no stopping me now. "And the engine runs other systems besides. There's—"

The woman's look really got to me. Patronized I didn't need to be. Not when I was the one and only aviator type around. I was about to say something unkind when I felt a hand on my arm. "Do not be defensive," Sandrine whispered. "Pandora thinks you are underestimating her skill, and that is not a wise thing to do. She is our finest artisan when it comes to mechanical matters."

"Whatever." I tossed the woman the keys. "Your call, lady. You'll have it done by tomorrow, right?"

That brought a laugh, and I managed to grin back. Fence mending had begun . . . maybe.

"We can use this time," Sandrine said, tugging at my arm. "Come with me."

I hadn't handled a sword since my days in the Corps, when I marched with the ceremonial troops in D.C. That NCO's sword had a chrome-plated blade, sharp only in appearance. Order arms, port arms, present arms; those maneuvers I could do as snappily as the next man. True, when I stood at attention in my parade blues and snapped the sword up in an arc to slap against my shoulder, it was all I could do not to wince; but it looked neat as hell. Then one evening, nursing beers in the slopchute, Gunny Bellows told me a secret: "I tape a Kotex pad between my blouse and my shoulder to absorb the blow."

I saw an opening and joked, "You know, Gunny, in boot camp we always wondered if you DI's wore Kotex." I wouldn't have been surprised if he poured his brew over my head; instead, he laughed his papa bear roar and threw an arm around me. His intimidation days were over.

"You are smiling," Sandrine said over lunch. "That is good . . . considering what lies before us."

"I was thinking about one time back in the—" There was no word for Marine Corps, but I managed to find a reasonable facsimile.

"You were a warrior then?" Suddenly she seemed optimistic.

"More a lover than a fighter, I'll admit now—but only to you. A running joke would be to tell a girl we were trying to impress that our hands were registered with the authorities as deadly weapons."

"Oh? And did they believe you?"

"Only when we were buying the drinks."

She laughed, a sound like wind chimes.

"Nice to see you smile, Sandrine. Smiles look good on you. You were grinning so wide in the plane I thought you were going to swallow your ears."

"Very funny. Finish your meal, and we shall go outside to the drill field."

"You're serious about teaching me how to use a sword?"

"Of course, I am serious. Aldenwalker, in the event we disturb a sleeping gorgon, we shall have to dispatch it quickly and silently."

"I wear a knife strapped to the calf of my jump suit, I can use that if need be."

"Think: to use a knife you would have to get much closer to the gorgon than you would with a sword. And you do not want to be that close to a gorgon, believe me."

Based upon her description of them, I realized that might be a very good point.

"Understood. Then lay on, Macduff, and damned be him that first cries, 'Hold, enough!'"

She shook her head. "Sometimes you say some very strange things."

Chapter 14

Everyone at the keep, it seemed, was an expert with the sword. Fencing was the sport of choice here, which proves that Abner Doubleday never made it to Alter Earth. Sandrine herself swung one mean saber, and time after time I found myself with a hard metal ball pressed against my chest hard enough to leave a bruise. She kept reminding me I needed to become proficient, and I kept reminding myself it was no sin to be out-swashbuckled by a woman. Sandrine would probably be right at home in a Hollywood pirate film. As one of the pirates. Hell, as their queen.

Days passed, and every now and then we'd go down to check on the progress of the engine rebuild, and every time we'd get the brush-off from Pandora and her crew. But it was more good-natured now—I would remind her that I remembered from my college lit classes that her name meant "bringer of woe" and get a laugh—and we developed a kind of rapport despite our dueling egos.

And dueling was something I was finally feeling pretty good about, occasionally even getting the better of my beautiful if intimidating opponent. Once I managed to center the tip of my blade on her left breast. She stood still, I pressed a little harder, and the ball nearly disappeared. "You did that on purpose," she said, barely breathing hard.

"It's a guy thing," I answered, and she shook her head and appeared to look away. She affected a hint of a smile as she turned back and said, "One more match?" Then, without warning, she effortlessly twirled her sword so fast it was a blur, and demonstrated how easily she could have had me singing in the soprano section.

She held the tip of her saber in its rather delicate position, flashed a grin, and said, "It is a girl thing."

By reference to the phases of the man-in-the-moon-less moon, I figured it was nearly a month—make that a lune—before Oreste announced over lunch that the engine modifications were finally complete and we could leave the next day. "Every day we wait is one day closer to the day the gorgons learn to use the equipment in the seaside keep. Once they have mastered that, we are doomed. I do not exaggerate." My boot camp training was obviously over—without even a graduation ceremony.

Evidently, Sandrine and Oreste had worked out their differences about her decision to be my *army of one,* although neither of them spoke about it to me or in front of me. I didn't know how she'd convinced him to see things her way, but it was none of my business. Having trained with her, I knew she would be as formidable a foe as any man. If Sergeant Bellows had a counterpart on Alter Earth, it was Sandrine. But she didn't spout profanities, she never berated me in drill instructor fashion, and she was one heck of a lot better to look at besides.

Pandora and her mechanics stood proudly nearby that afternoon as Oreste popped open the cowling's inspection port—and I almost fell over. The *engine* they had put inside looked like a steel beach ball with a prop shaft coming out the front. Two feed tubes led into the back, evidently for the Power supply and the gold catalyst. There were some more wires and conduits whose purpose was foreign to me (no surprise), and on the underside was a slab of rock, cut to fit and fastened in place. "Ballast," noted Oreste, and Pandora laughed and punched me in the shoulder.

The original engine sat close by, and containers next to it held the gas from the Cessna's wing tanks.

Pandora showed me inside the cabin and pointed to the throttle. "It is simpler than before," she said.

"Push in on the plunger and the puller turns; pull out and it stops turning." I could appreciate that. "Also, I was not comfortable with the airship's braking mechanism."

"Welcome to the club."

She ignored me. "I noticed that your puller—"

"That's called a propeller," I said. She looked dismissively at me.

"Your puller can change its pitch, as you know. Greater pitch to lift the ship, lesser to keep it flying more efficiently. Now, note this mark on the plunger." She had etched a notch into the prop control stem near the knob on its end. "If you push past this point, the pitch will reverse and change from a puller to a pusher. It will help the brakes to slow you after you land."

"Wow," I said, impressed beyond words. "Beta."

She frowned, probably recognizing the Greek and wondered how it applied. It didn't matter. The beta pitch would be a thrust reverser, something that might come in handy for a short-field landing.

Oreste told me upon the successful completion of the mission he'd have Pandora's crew restore everything as it was so I could return to my own world with the plane in the same condition as when I'd come over.

Sandrine put a hand on my arm and squeezed. We were both thinking the same thought, with the operational word being *successful.*

Chapter 15

Sunset fell upon the seaside keep. The plateau stood as smooth and flat as it had been more than two thousand years ago. The bordering mountain keep, with its sliding doors that opened into a once-thriving scientific outpost, was still. The only sound was that of a freshwater spring as it trickled down the mountainside into a pool at its base. No birds were there to bathe in the pool or drink from it. No snakes lay on the rocks, trying for one last moment's worth of warmth. No lizards scampered about looking for insects to eat.

One of the sliding doors stood open. From inside, another sound intruded upon the stillness of the scene—that of shuffling feet, and of objects being dragged. Soon two figures shambled out of the darkness, each hauling the dead and drained body of a human. The figures were gorgons, and they were females, obvious from the fact that unlike their male counterparts, they were without wings. Nature had played a cruel trick on the females, this denying them of wings, for it made them subservient to the males upon whom they largely depended for their sustenance. The entire gorgon social order, if social it could be called, was based upon male dominance.

Indeed, the only living things these females felt superior to were the living prey brought to them by their masters.

The females dragged the desiccated bodies to the end of the ancient runway, which dropped precipitously to the sea. Without ceremony, without giving their task any more thought than a human would give to taking out the trash, they pushed the bodies over the edge and turned away, not caring to watch them strike the rocks below and succumb to the ocean's embrace. Without a word to each other, they walked back to the cave to retrieve the next two bodies.

In the laboratory above the entry level, Ibliss, leader of the gorgons by dint of height, strength, and power to intimidate, leaned over the ancient texts that he knew were operational manuals. Try as he might, a translation simply would not come to him, and he badly wanted to learn how to make the bridge device function. He thirsted for the ability to pick his victims from the human village and span them to his lair without the inconvenience of staging a raid. Clever though they were, gorgons had—over the millennia since the War for Power—lost the need for written language. They passed on their culture and traditions, such as they were, verbally, in the language common to all on Alter Earth. But the written word had become foreign to them.

And thus Ibliss struggled to associate symbols with sounds.

A check in the makeshift mortuarium on the first level had revealed that six more humans had not survived the day. Those stupid females had still not gotten the equation right. Their task had been simple enough: strap the humans to their trays, inject a feeding tube in one arm and a drainage tube in the other; take out enough blood to keep them in a stupor, but feed them enough nutrients to keep them alive. Thus, the humans' bodies would remanufacture more blood to keep supply up to demand. It was an ingenious plan, one he might continue even after he had figured out how to use the bridge. He didn't want to obliterate the entire human population, after all. They were delicacies, and well worth preserving.

While in transit to their nocturnal raid on the other keep, the gorgons had noted the human settlement midway between, along a broad river. Excellent. He chuckled, imagining the surprise in that settlement on some future evening, when the humans saw one or more of their people simply disappear. There would be no hint of what had happened, or where they had gone—and no way to prepare for the next time, either. Or the next, or the next. They would live in a constant state of fear. And that was dearly to be desired. Fear had a taste all its own.

There was one problem, though, and one day— make that one night—he would need to solve that, too. The humans in the other keep would have to be dealt with, as they doubtless had devices similar to his own, knew how to use them, and could monitor his covey's movements. But they could not reach him now, because thanks to his raid, they no longer had enough of their precious Power to operate their machines for much longer; this much information he had managed to wrest from one of this keep's former occupants before committing him to a draining table.

Thoughts of draining brought another, less pleasant idea to mind. With six more humans dead, he would have to send six of his soldiers to the fennics to fly back replacements. Ibliss tolerated his distant evolutionary cousins—tolerated them at best; despised them at worst, which was whenever one stood in his presence. In that regard, he was no different from the rest of his kind, who saw in the short, round, strut-strut-strutting fennics an inflated sense of importance they hardly deserved. In fact, did not deserve at all.

But the fennics did possess humans, used as slaves when young, and as food when they grew too old or weak to serve. Ibliss would insist the fennics surrender only the healthiest to his *ambassadors*. The fennics would posture and protest, as was their wont, claiming the gorgons were taking their humans faster than the fennics could make them reproduce, but this was of no import to Ibliss, whether it was true or not.

Soon, Ibliss would master the bridging device, and he would span humans at will to the mortuarium. Then he would have no need for fennics—although he might play a little joke on them and steal all their humans, leaving his contemptible cousins to fend for themselves. Their blood—the fennics'—was simply too sour to make them worth draining. Except, of course, in an emergency.

Another thing he would enjoy doing was spanning that other group of humans to the mortuarium—the ones who lived in the far-away keep and from whom he and his minions had stolen their precious Power. Yes. He would have great fun with them.

Chapter 16

From Oreste's description, I surmised the distance between the two keeps was about two hundred miles, an easy hour-and-a-half flight in the Skylane. Or it would've been, had we flown direct. Oreste had other plans, however, which he detailed that afternoon as we looked at the newly modified Skylane.

"Fly south toward the edge of this plateau," he advised. "There the land drops sharply to the barrens."

"I remember flying over desert when I got here, before reaching this plateau. To say it's steep and deep would be a serious understatement."

"A remnant from the cataclysm. You must fly below the escarpment and along it toward the west."

"Got it. Stay low and hide from the gorgons, in case they're looking."

Oreste looked annoyed with my butting in. I guessed it was understandable; after all, tomorrow he'd be sending his own daughter into the jaws of death. Literally. That could probably make one testy. I decided just to shut up and let him continue.

"The drop is immense, true, but it grows less and less as you travel west and the land rises. Eventually, you will reach a waterfall where the river that flows behind the mountain here drops onto the barrens. The cliff is low at that point, but the mountains rising beyond should provide adequate cover. Fly until you reach the ocean and approach the keep from the sea. If the gorgons happen to be looking, chances are it will not be in that direction."

"Sounds like a plan," I said.

That evening, we reviewed our strategy—our approach to the other keep, the probable location of the stolen casks, the bomb and its remote-controlled detonator that Sandrine would activate once we were safely in the plane and on our way back. Then we reviewed it again. And again. Finally, yawning even though I knew sleep would be long in coming, I announced it was time for me to hit the hay.

Father and daughter stared at each other blankly. "What?" asked Oreste.

"Why would you strike at the animals' food?"

"Sandrine, it's an expression. It means go to bed."

"Then why do you not say that?"

"And why do you people not use contractions? Look, it's an idiom, a figure of speech. We use them all the time where I come from."

Sandrine raised her eyebrows as she observed, unnecessarily I might add, "Aldenwalker, you are no longer where you come from."

The next morning dawned bright, as usual. But a check outside showed high cumulus clouds were forming to our west, which could indicate the type of frontal system that more often than not brings thunderstorms with it. I explained that to Oreste and suggested we wait a day for the front to pass. He said no; we'd waited long enough already. Every day's delay meant another day's progress by the gorgons in learning to use the technology they'd commandeered. Back on my world, it's the pilot who has final say, but as I'd been reminded, I was no longer on my world. Plus, the old man—I mean, Oreste—had a point.

"You look dashing," said Sandrine, tongue firmly in cheek, as the two of us sat down to breakfast, sat down to what could very well be our last meal on this or any other Earth. I'd put on my one-piece saffron-colored jump suit for the occasion, with the sheath knife strapped to my calf as usual. The knife was standard equipment, intended for jump emergencies: in the event of a malfunction, it would allow me to cut away the malfing chute before deploying the reserve. It avoided the danger of the emergency chute's getting tangled in the lines of the other. Fortunately, I'd never had to use it.

Lynda wouldn't wear a knife. Teased me with, "You Tarzan, me Jane." But that particular exchange never occurred in the books. Her experience with Burroughs was strictly through the movies, which was not really Burroughs at all.

"I said, you look dashing," Sandrine repeated, and I came back to the present. Her head was cocked, and that glimmer of a grin teased me. "Especially since you have decided to look like a man instead of a boy."

I had given up shaving after about a week. "When in Rome," I said. "An old saying on my world."

"I would remind you—"

"But you don't have to. And what makes you so *up* this morning? In a few minutes we'll be flying into . . ." I let my words trail off. Her father had joined us, and he looked even less comfortable with our assignment now the task was finally upon us.

"That is why I am so *up* this morning, whatever that means. Because we shall be flying."

"Oh. And by the way, you look dashing, too." Actually, she did look pretty fetching in her own tight coverall, which was the same olive-and-copper color as her skin. Against a background of forest or rock, she would be pretty well camouflaged; me, I'd stand out like a robed Buddhist monk at a busy airport.

"Thank you, Aldenwalker. Good morning, old man."

Oreste nodded. "I still wish you had not insisted to be the one to go on this mission," he said—to his daughter, not to me. Not that my feelings were hurt, mind you. "Sandrine, do not—I repeat, do not—cause me to lose the last member of my family."

"And as we have discussed, that is why I am going. I have the best reason to go—and in you, the best reason to return. Please do not give me the lecture again, old man. I shall keep my perspective, and if I do overreact, I have Aldenwalker here to correct me." She said *correct*, not *protect*.

"For the record," I interjected, "Alden and Walker are two names, not one. The second is my family name. I mean, you can call me by either name and I'll answer, but you don't have to call me by both. Understand?"

Sandrine considered it. "I understand . . . Aldenwalker."

"Never mind." Actually, I was beginning to like it. And I cautioned myself against calling her Sandy in return (or retaliation). This girl—*don't call her a* girl *either, Walker*—was a true steel magnolia, a quality I had come to admire more and more in certain women I'd come to know. In that regard, she was a lot like Lynda.

Plus, she was far better than I was with a sword.

Chapter 17

I carried our swords to the plane and tossed them into the luggage compartment on top of my parachute pack, which I'd never removed. Sandrine reached into the glove box on the instrument panel, where I kept my first aid kit, and put next to it a container holding a small explosive device—a baby's handful of Power and a gram or so of gold. The gold was encased in a protective coating and buried inside the Power. When the timer—also inside the tiny container—was remotely activated, a chemical would dissolve the coating, allowing the catalyst to react with the reagent, and boom. Bye-bye, gorgons—if everything went according to plan.

I wondered if anyone in this universe had ever heard of Mr. Murphy and his infallible Law.

Oreste embraced Sandrine and seemed unwilling to let go, but the sun was climbing above the horizon, and we had to get a move on. When he released her, I extended my hand. He looked at it. "Why are you showing me your hand?"

"On my world, it's how people say hello or good-bye. They shake hands."

"Oh." He held out his hand and shook it up and down and side to side. It looked ridiculous.

"No, no, like this." And I grabbed his hand and gave it a proper shake. "It's a mark of respect and friendship and—um, good will."

"Ah." He nodded. "Then I shall be happy to shake hands. Bring my daughter back safely."

"Old man," reminded Sandrine, "perhaps it is I who will bring Aldenwalker back safely."

We hopped into the Cessna, secured the doors, and strapped in. The plane was facing into the breeze, and in front of us was clear flat land. "All set?" I asked. Sandrine gave me that smile I've seen countless times on new student pilots, except hers was far prettier. I made sure the prop pitch was in takeoff mode, and then I pushed the throttle in about a quarter inch. The plane shot forward so fast I thought the propeller would yank itself off and fly away on its own. I jerked the throttle back and voiced an expression that I normally wouldn't use in the presence of a lady.

Sandrine turned to me. "How can excrement be sacred?" she asked, frowning.

"Sorry," I said. "Just another quaint idiom from my world—which I am no longer on; thank you very much for not reminding me."

She looked forward and without asking, placed her fingers on the yoke and the toes of her boots against the rudder pedals. I checked the operation of the controls—ailerons, elevator, rudder—and very slowly this time pushed the throttle forward, a millimeter at a time. The propeller spun, Two Four Quebec built up groundspeed in no time, and when the airspeed indicator reached sixty-five I pulled back on the yoke, the nose rose, and we were airborne.

On a parachutist's first jump, immediately after the chute opens, his first surprise—aside from the fact he is still alive—is the silence. He is floating, like a disembodied spirit, half a mile or so above the ground. Nothing that makes noise is any closer than that, with the possible exception of the fluttering of the parachute's hem if there's a breeze. It is almost absolutely still, and that blend of serenity and exhilaration is what makes many a jumper come back for more. That was what I felt now. Serene, exhilarated, and free from the drone of engine noise.

At altitude I adjusted the prop for cruise pitch, fine-tuned the trim, and let Sandrine fly the plane. After a few minutes, I coached her in climbs and descents, and when we reached the abrupt border of high land and low, I let her take us below the ridge-line. She learned to make pretty well coordinated turns using aileron and rudder, and holding altitude was becoming easier for her. She was a natural, and she was loving it.

Until the storm came. *Thanks, Oreste. Hello, Murphy.*

I saw the dark clouds fast approaching and with them a flash of lightning. Sandrine motioned to me, and I took hold of my yoke as she released hers. I climbed and turned us toward the plateau again. No way would I risk landing on desert sand. The first large drops of rain were spattering against the wind-shield when I found a large grassy clearing suitable for landing. I bounced the plane in, braked with feet and reverse pitch, and reminded my passenger, rather sheepishly, that any landing you can walk away from is a good one.

The squall passed us quickly, and I opened the doors to air out the cabin. Sandrine left to relieve herself in the woods, and I figured it was a good time to make a pit stop myself. She walked in one direction as I headed in another. I was glad to see it. It's a holdover from my childhood: bathroom time is private. That's why there's only one seat in the head. Unless you're French, and that other one doesn't count, does it?

I wandered into the woods a few feet and watered a tree, then headed back for the clearing—but was halted in my tracks by a welcome discovery on the forest floor: strawberries. Not just any strawberries, strawberries as big as oranges. Wow, I thought, as I drew my knife and squatted to cut one into sections. Won't Sandrine enjoy—

A sound made me freeze. Movement in the woods behind me. A snort. I looked around and found myself facing a unicorn, definitely not a domesticated one. Its head was down, and its corkscrew horn was aimed at my chest. It snorted again, and blood foamed from its nostrils. Something that looked like an arrow pro-truded from its neck.

It charged.

Chapter 18

I flew into the air as the knife fell from my fingers. Straight up I went, and the unicorn passed beneath, its horn nearly grazing my foot. Something had gripped my arms and lifted me above the ground. Not something, I realized as I twisted my head first to one side and then the other, but someone; or more accurately, two someones.

They were men, kind of, brown and covered with short fur, with long arms, narrow faces, and lipless mouths. They held me by my upper arms, and their free hands pulled us through the trees effortlessly, with complete synchronicity. It was one of those Harry Hairbreadth moments you see in 1930s-era serials, but this rescue wasn't staged for a camera. The unicorn was real. My benefactors, who- or whatever they were, were also real. And my near death was real, too. Too real.

Sandrine. Where was she now? Did she see what happened? Would she follow me? And where would she follow me to? These guys weren't just hanging around waiting for some dumb shlub to save. They had a destination, and they were headed for it, holding me between them and not saying a word, not even looking at me.

They dropped me unceremoniously on a platform beside a tree house and disappeared back into the forest. Didn't even give me the chance to thank them.

The platform was about six feet by nine, secured between the branches about ten feet above the ground, and covered with ferns. The house looked like a tipi covered with leaves, and as I stood up I thought I heard movement from behind a closed flap.

"Hello?" I called across the platform. "Anybody home?"

The flap moved, and I saw a hand. It was black and glossy as sable, with long, delicate fingers. It pushed the flap open, and a woman emerged.

Her face was beautiful, framing the most arresting pair of golden eyes. Those eyes held mine fast as she stared into them. A moment more, and she glided leisurely across the platform, her arms extended.

Slowly, as if she were some computer-generated effect, the woman seemed to morph. Her eyes became green. Her face grew pink, with a sprinkle of freckles across her nose. Her hair was red and long. She smiled, and dimples formed in her cheeks.

I whispered a name, and it came out a question. My mind said it couldn't be, but my eyes told me it couldn't *not* be. There she was, in the flesh, naked and pure and reaching out to me, and I entered her embrace. She frowned as her fingers fumbled with the jumpsuit's zipper that ran from my neck to my crotch. *Funny,* a part of me thought to her, *you've worn jumpsuits every weekend for the past eight months, and now you act like you're seeing one for the first time.* She found the tab, pulled it all the way down, and her smile returned, my lovely little leprechaun.

We lowered ourselves to the fern-covered platform and made love. Lynda pulled me toward her, her wide-open eyes holding me as strongly as her arms. Faintly, so faint and far away it could've been my imagination, I heard my name being called; my first and last together, as if it were one name and one name only.

Suddenly Lynda morphed again. Her skin darkened to somewhere between copper and olive. Her lips were lush, her eyes almond-shaped and the color of coal, her casually cropped short hair black as night. It lasted but a second, and suddenly she was Lynda again, and I was helpless to resist, and when the moment came I cried out her name and exploded inside her.

My jumpsuit was still on, my shorts yanked low. This was not how I'd pictured my wedding night, our first lovemaking as man and wife. The line between love and lust had blurred, along with my perception of what was real and what was . . . not.

Lynda rolled me over onto my back and kissed my belly as I buried my fingers in her auburn hair. She moved up to my chest, my neck, my lips. She smiled broadly then, and there was something odd, something decidedly un-Lynda, about that smile. Then she kissed my neck again. I felt two pinches on the side of my throat.

Not pinches. Punctures.

I yelped and tried to pull away, but it was impossible to move. When did Lynda become so strong? I felt my vitality drain, felt an overwhelming lethargy sweep over me like a warm wave in the summer surf. My hand was no longer in Lynda's fine red hair; it was entangled in sleek black fur. I passed out.

When I came to, the world was upside down. No, that would be me who was upside down. And bound. Bound! My feet had been fastened by a length of white cord to a branch above me, leaving my head hanging some three feet above the platform. My arms were pinned to my sides. I was wrapped chest to toe like a mummy, except these weren't flat cotton strips; they were more like twine, or maybe a moist and sticky white webbing. My head throbbed, and the punctures on my neck hurt worse than before, probably inflamed.

I felt like a caterpillar inside a cocoon. Or a fly in a—

Did I say webbing? Oh, Lord.

I didn't know how she had done what she did, but I suddenly knew why my two rescuers had put me here. They represented the male of the species, and one of them had been slated to . . .

I was his substitute. And he got to live another day.

The tipi flap opened, and for the first time I saw the woman for who—for what—she was. She was still compelling, in a feral sort of way, and she was still naked. But my eyes weren't fixed this time on her golden orbs. Nor were they held by the curved mandibles at the edges of her open-mouthed smile. Instead, something else attracted them, something much lower.

It was the bright red hourglass in the middle of her glossy black belly.

Chapter 19

Sandrine shucked her coveralls and undergar-
ments and squatted behind a tree. For some reason,
she had always been modest about eliminating her
waste. It was not logical; the process was, after all,
a natural function. Maybe, she thought, it had to do
with her waste functions' bordering on what her oh-so-
shy mother had referred to as her *pleasure portal.* Like
mother, like daughter? Sandrine had never thought
herself a prude, but still . . . Ander had laughed at her
idiosyncrasy, and at her refusal even to be in the same
room when he himself voided. But he humored her, as
he often did, without comment or complaint, and she
had loved him dearly.

Once the couple thought she had conceived, and
the joy in their union seemed complete. But then her
lunar cycle returned, and Sandrine was crestfallen.
Ander, no less despondent, had directed his energies
toward cheering her. He said that the process was as
important as the product, and he promised to continue the process even after his seed had taken root.
Just to keep in practice.

Aldenwalker had asked if she laid eggs.

With a shake of her head, Sandrine came back
to the present. She cleaned herself with some leaves,
rubbed her hands against the tree trunk, and hiked up
her coveralls. Aldenwalker, she thought. A stranger in
a strange land. She would be furious in his situation,
furious at being so manipulated, so out of control of
his own destiny. This was not his fight, it was hers;
her people's. Yet he seemed to accept his lot with a
certain grace, a certain fatalism. What will be, will be.

He had told her nothing about himself, except that he too had lost his consort, and Sandrine had been too proper—not to mention preoccupied with more pressing matters, like his swordsmanship training—to pry. In principle, his own history ultimately did not matter; as her father reminded her regularly, outside his hearing, it was of no moment. His humanity aside—she had to smile at his quirky but somehow charming way of mangling speech by pushing so many of his words together, making one word out of two—Aldenwalker was simply a means to an end, that of helping to return the Power to its rightful owners and to destroy the gorgons. Once that was done, Oreste would return him to his own world, his own dimension, and he would be gone forever. Returning with a story he could tell no one, for who would believe him?

She also thought she remembered learning in passing, long ago, about there being a temporal bridge as well as a spatial one . . .

The airship stood there on its three wheels, tail high, doors open, looking poised to fly. Would she miss the flying as much as she would miss Aldenwalker?

Sandrine brought herself up short. Would she, in fact, miss Aldenwalker? Part of her, she admitted, would, if only for the fact she had grown used to having him around over the past lune. But she missed him now for a more immediate reason. The airship was empty, and he was nowhere to be seen.

Something bolted from the forest a distance away. It stopped short and staggered back into the woods. A unicorn. That was the direction Aldenwalker had gone. She ran to the place, looked from side to side, and saw nothing. Then she looked down and saw his sheath knife on the ground. She slipped it inside her coveralls, stepped over a patch of strawberries, and bolted into the forest.

Sandrine grew anxious. They needed to be on their way. The squall had slowed them down already, and the morning was nearly gone. She called his name once, loudly, and heard no response. But seconds later, two brown-furred humanoids dropped from the trees.

She had never seen arachnids; but from her studies as a girl, she knew what they were. And she remembered how they lived, and how they typically died.

Her sword was still in the plane. She reached for the knife inside her coveralls, but from somewhere on his body one of the arachnids shot a strand of webbing that wrapped itself around her waist. It pinned the knife against her body, and before she knew what was happening, Sandrine found herself tied to the trunk of a tree with more of the sticky cords.

The arachnids leered at her, hooked mandibles protruding from the sides of their mouths, their sex organs engorged with the ichor that passed in their bodies for blood. Sandrine feared not only for her body and psyche, but also for her life itself. Once they had used her, they would likely dispose of her. Or leave her tied to the tree, where any manner of predator or scavenger could finish her off. And her vital mission would die with her.

She knew where men were most vulnerable, and perhaps the arachnids shared that trait. There was nothing to do but try, but first she had to get free of her bonds. Sandrine stopped her struggles, stared at the arachnids, and smiled. They blinked and stopped in their tracks. She nodded toward their midsections and said, "If I had known your intentions, I would not have resisted. Forgive me."

The two, still silent—perhaps they were incapable of speech—relaxed.

"I would love to share my body with you," Sandrine went on. Her voice was soft and seductive now, and if her tormentors did not understand her words, her tone left no doubt as to intent. "But I cannot please you fully while I am fastened to this tree. I really need both my hands free." She nodded toward her bindings. "Would you, please?"

Each arachnid looked at the other, as if waiting for his companion to make the move. Finally, one walked to the tree and, with a fingernail, snapped the cord. His partner removed the sticky binding from Sandrine's waist. "Thanks to you both," she cooed. They took a step back, gauging her next move. Would she try to escape? Foolish female if she did; they could easily recapture her, and this time the binding would stay put.

But she did not run. Sandrine reached her hands up and stroked the fur on the sides of the arachnids' faces. Her fingertips beneath their chins urged them closer, and she ran her hands down their bodies in sweetly seductive movements. "I hope you are ready for me, my friends," she said as she lowered herself to her knees and dug the toes of her boots into the earth behind her for purchase. The arachnids looked down as she slid her hands up the insides of their legs, and then they tilted their heads back in anticipation of what was to come.

But what came was not what they were expecting. Sandrine slid her fingers down their legs again, as if teasing them. Then she balled her hands into fists, took careful aim, and slammed up into them with all her strength. Two hissing screams burst from their mouths, and as Sandrine jumped to her feet, they fell to the ground. They held onto themselves in agony, and one began to vomit.

Sandrine knew instinctively she should draw the knife from her coveralls and kill the arachnids as they lay helpless and writhing on the ground. For a reason she couldn't explain, she didn't; instead, she ran into the woods, searching and calling for Aldenwalker. But there was no trail for her to follow. After running for a long time, she burst out of the forest and into a clearing—not fifty yards from where the airship stood, untouched and still alone.

She'd been running in a circle.

Chapter 20

Blood filled my empty head as I hung helpless from the widow's webbing. She approached me, a pointed black tongue licking the sides of her lipless mouth. How could I have seen beauty in this predator? Yet, there were those eyes . . .

Stop it, Walker, you're starting to see her *again. And* she *isn't here. She's deep in the ground, in another dimension, on another world.*

The creature stepped closer. Drool dribbled from her mouth. I had to do something. But what? I was mummified. I couldn't move. Except—

I scrunched up my body as if I were doing a sit-up, then relaxed my abs. She stopped, curious, watching me. I repeated the inverted sit-up, again and again, initiating a swinging motion that I hoped would be enough to break the cord that held me and let me fall—although what I would do after I did fall hadn't crossed my mind.

It worked, sort of. At least I got a swing started. Maybe she had never seen one of her entrées do this before; maybe her meals had just given in; or maybe my struggles merely amused her. Nevertheless, she let me swing back and forth for a bit until she got tired of it and reached for me with an expression on her face that made me shiver. I was on the backswing then, and as I came forward, my head was directly in line with her red hourglass. She grabbed my hips to stop me, but I bent forward—lunged, actually—and pressed my face into that red spot.

And bit. Hard.

A shriek that sounded like a siren pierced my ears, and I felt her hands try to push me away. But I wouldn't, I couldn't, let go. I needed to hold fast to her, in spite of the foul-smelling ooze that gurgled around my teeth and threatened to choke me. Keep pushing on me, bitch, I thought as I fought to keep from coughing. Keep the pressure on.

And she did. She pushed so hard that the cord broke and we tumbled through the branches to land with a thud on the ground. We were no longer attached, but she continued shrieking, and I realized that part of her torn body was still in my mouth. I spit it out. Red fur covered a clump of greenish gore, barely inches from my face. I lay on my side, still bound, still helpless, one ear to the earth.

The widow stood up, stared at the hole my teeth had made in her abdomen, and intensified her shrieking. My ears actually hurt from it; at least the one that wasn't pressed to the ground. She looked back at me, and black venom dripped from her mandibles. She took a step forward, then another, and I knew I was doomed.

My ear, the one pressed to the ground, sensed a vibration, one that quickly grew stronger. Suddenly, the widow was jerked upright. Her belly was pushed forward from the inside, and a corkscrew horn drove through her. It pulled her into the air and slammed her to the earth, again and again, before she and her attacker finally fell down in death.

The unicorn: the one with the bolt in its neck; the one that had narrowly missed skewering me. It had finally found something upon which to vent its fury.

Breathing wasn't easy in my cocoon, but at least the blood had flowed back from my head and left some room for thought. If I could manage to crawl to the horn and wedge it between my body and the webbing, maybe it could be snapped.

There was no way I could use my hands. I felt like a worm, or a snake, but I didn't have the internal crawling mechanisms they did. And in my mummy wraps, I was starting to get claustrophobic.

Crawl, Walker, I commanded myself; I wiggled forward, drawing up my knees and pushing with my feet until I managed to insinuate the horn between the back of my neck and the webbing. I pushed forward, my face closer and closer to that repugnant countenance with its sharp mandibles . . .

The horn trick didn't work. I just couldn't exert enough pressure to snap the bonds. But then I saw the widow's mandibles again. Her mouth was wide open, and they were extended, poised to attack or defend. I wriggled back off the horn and toward those blades. *Careful,* I thought, *there's venom there.*

Slowly, I inched my way to a mandible and squirmed against it just enough to slice through the first strand of cord. Then another, and another. Finally, I was able to cut enough to free one arm, and from that point—no pun intended—it was relatively short work to free myself completely. But I was trembling when I was done, and soaked through with sweat.

Sandrine, I thought. *Where the hell were you through all this? Didn't you notice I was gone? Hello?*

Stop it, Walker. You're an idiot. There could be any number of reasons she didn't follow you—a principal one being that she never saw you disappear in the first place and wouldn't know where to begin to look.

Having finished beating myself up, I pulled up my shorts, zipped up my jump suit, and began looking for a way out of the forest.

Chapter 21

I couldn't retrace my steps, because I hadn't taken any steps. The spiders—and why didn't Oreste or Sandrine warn me about the spiders?—had taken me through the trees, and that made backtracking difficult. They had made a kind of straight line from the edge of the forest to the widow's lair, so I looked up at the platform, plotted a reverse course, and began walking.

From far away, I thought I heard a woman's voice calling my name. "Sandrine!" I shouted, got a response, and a few minutes later, we were hugging each other in relief.

"What happened to you?" she asked, and when I told her she shook her head. "A widow! No one escapes a widow's embrace."

"Yeah, I've been meaning to ask you about that," I said, "but first, what happened to you?"

She told me, and it was my turn to wince. "Let's get back to the plane," I said.

"It is growing late," Sandrine said. "Perhaps we should return to the keep for tonight and try again tomorrow."

"You know? That's not a bad idea. Let's go."

But when we got back to the clearing another surprise awaited us. Those two spiders again. But this time, they were rummaging around in the plane, and when they heard my shout they jumped out—one carrying a sword and the other holding my parachute pack. They ran for the woods, and without a second thought I ran after them.

They split up at the border of the woods and were about to take to the trees when one of them, the one with my parachute under one arm, was jerked backwards with a force that caused him to leave the ground, to fall on his back—with a bolt, like the one in the unicorn's neck, through his chest. I ran up and grabbed the chute, ran after the one carrying my sword, and was brought up short.

And by short, I mean short. As in people, but not people. A group of brown-furred, beady-eyed, barrel-shaped beasts, naked but armed with spears, knives, and crossbows. Some were carrying the butchered carcass of what could have been the unicorn which had inadvertently saved my life—only to plunk me down into a new crisis, one involving a hunting party of what looked like humanoid rats.

They had captured the other spider, who was trembling, and one of them was holding the sword.

"That's mine," I said, hoping they understood and would let me go in peace.

Hah. Fat chance.

"Take him," one said, one nearly as tall as I; and wrinkled pink fingers grabbed me around the arms and held me fast. "How did you escape?" the leader asked, and I looked at him dumbly, something I was becoming very proficient at.

"I don't know what you're talking about," I said. "Let me go and I'll leave you alone."

They found that enormously funny.

"Who are you?" the leader demanded. "I am Ulm."

I decided to Geneva Convention him. "Walker, Alden James. Corporal, United States Marine Corps. Serial number—oof!" I'd caught the butt of a spear in the belly. Obviously, they'd never heard of prisoner's rights. "All right, I'll make it simple. I'm . . . an offworlder."

Another funny joke. These guys loved to laugh.

"Bring him to Scud," said Ulm. "Our traps have produced more than unicorn meat today."

Instead of heading for the clearing, we marched in column through the woods until we came to the edge of the great cliff, with my humble person flanked and held firmly by two of the hunting party. I looked out and saw nothing but desert, thousands upon thousands of feet below. The spider dude (I couldn't bring myself to think of him as Spiderman) had been marched in front of me, and every so often one of these little rats poked at him with a spear point. His back was sporting a score of pus-colored rivulets by the time we reached the cliff.

Ulm nodded, and one of his party grabbed the arachnid's ankles while the other grabbed his wrists. He shrieked, his call sounding much like the stricken widow's, which was enough to make my skin crawl all over again. The rat folk cringed, too; evidently their hearing was more sensitive. "On my mark," called Ulm, and the guards swung the spider over the edge, then let him swing back. Out he went again, and back. "Ready," called Ulm, and with the next swing he shouted, "Go!"

Out the spider went, but at the last second he shot a strand of webbing and snagged one of the rats with it. He was yanked screaming over the edge with the spider, and the two spun around each other like an eight-spoked pinwheel as they fell. The rat-man's screams faded as they dropped, and I mentally ticked off the time, a skydiver's habit, until their bodies struck the ground below. It took nearly fifty seconds 'til impact.

The others stood still, as if shocked at the loss of their man. Then Ulm exploded in laughter and the others quickly joined in. "Ho! That's a good joke on Orr!" They laughed long and loud. And then they turned to me.

Gulp.

"Why did you do that?" I asked Ulm.

"Too stringy, too bitter," he said, spitting. "Nothing at all like you."

Chapter 22

The rat-like creatures pushed me along the cliff face until we came to a ledge leading to a cavern whose huge opening lay some twenty feet below. They were greeted by a host of surly females who relieved the males of their unicorn chunks. They were about to make off with them when they noticed me. I had been kept to the rear of the line, but now was shoved to the fore. The females stopped what they were doing and stared. Little rat-brats ran up and started pulling at my jumpsuit until they were kicked aside by the men.

The one called Ulm barked an order to a female and she went scurrying as the brats shouted taunts at me—at a safe distance from the males' feet. She returned with a rat even larger than Ulm in tow. This one wore a broad swordbelt, and his teeth when he smiled reminded me of a lumber mill. He looked at me and beetled his brow as Ulm spoke a few words to him.

"So, human, my subchief tells me you claim to be an offworlder. You expect me to believe that myth?"

"The widow didn't believe it either," I said. "Ask old Ulm what happened to her."

They conferred, and the chief assumed a somewhat different expression. "My name is Scud," he said. "What business do you have with the fennics?"

Fennics. The word meant nothing to me. "No business at all," I replied. "Two arachnids stole my belongings—my sword and my—um, travel pack. I was trying to get them back when your boys found me and dragged me here against my will."

"Hmm. And how did you happen to find yourself in our land in the first place?"

I borrowed from Burroughs and said, "I have no idea. I fell asleep on my world and woke up here. Just yesterday, in fact. And I'd been wandering around, kind of orienting myself, when I stumbled upon the widow."

"Uh huh." I admit my story wasn't convincing, and Scud's snarl confirmed that. "Your name, offworlder?"

"Alden Walker."

"What's in your pack?"

"Some changes of clothes. I'd been hiking."

"Slaves don't wear clothes."

Slaves? Slaves? The implication sent a cold thrill up my spine. These . . . things . . . had slaves? Human slaves?

Scud took my sword from the fennic who'd been carrying it.

"Yours, too?" he said. I nodded. "You didn't escape from here, did you?"

"I'm not a slave. My world knows no such things as slaves." That's me, ever the idealist.

"The world of the fennics does. Until they get too old to be useful, that is. Then . . ." A trickle of spittle escaped from one side of his mouth. It took all my effort to keep my face impassive.

Scud studied me with his beady black eyes and spoke to Ulm. "He doesn't look like one of ours," he said. "Look at his pale skin. Our slaves don't have light hair and blue eyes, either." He leaned forward and sniffed me, wrinkled his pointy nose, and seemed satisfied. "If anyone qualifies as an offworlder, it would be this one."

"Maybe he tells the truth," suggested Ulm. Scud nodded, slowly, as if still considering.

"I'd really like to go now," I said, trying to affect an air of confidence.

The fennics laughed again, as if I'd just told them the world's dirtiest joke.

"You've got balls," said Scud, "I'll give you that. Who knows? Only an offworlder would be so stupid as to make a remark like that." He put a hairy arm around my shoulders. "We have much to consider, offworlder. But for now, I'm hungry. You'll join us." The fennics looked at each other and murmured amongst themselves. I thought I heard someone suggest I might taste as exotic as I looked. "Give him back his sword. We'll treat this human as, oh, as a guest. For now."

This brought more gales of laughter. From everyone but me.

Dinner was served by slaves, and it was all I could do to keep my outrage in check. In the mid-nineteenth century, I'd probably have joined John Brown's rebellion—and been hanged alongside him.

These slaves were surely of Sandrine's species; in other words, Alter Earth humans: dusky skin, dark hair, almond eyes. They were filthy and emaciated, recalling images from Auschwitz. Moreover, they were denied the dignity of clothing. The fennics wore no clothes, just harnesses for their hunting and fighting gear, so to them this would be no big deal. Probably the slaves didn't give it a second thought either, now, as they shuffled about, totally dehumanized, wordlessly performing their duties.

No plates sat on the long tables. A portion of cooked meat was simply placed before each fennic, who slavered and slobbered over it as he jammed it between his jaws. The females, sitting at separate tables, displayed similar manners. Obviously, there were no ladies in the room.

An elderly slave presented a piece of meat to me, and I caught a flicker of surprise before he lowered his eyes again. I wished I were in a position to help him. More, I wished there were a Spartacus among them. One with better luck than the original.

The sounds of gnashing and noshing and crude conversation took on a white noise aspect as I pulled at the tough meat. It was stringy and tasted like nothing I'd ever eaten on Earth—tangy and gamey, with none of the sweetness natural fat would provide. The closest I could come to approximate the taste was to think of undercooked venison, but that would be the most distant of gustatory cousins. I managed to get it down, but only because I was starving.

Was Sandrine starving as well? If she were smart, she'd fill up on those strawberries I'd found, maybe find some other edibles in other bushes, and then lock herself in the airplane overnight. Tomorrow, if I could engineer a proper exit, I'd make my way back to her.

If: the biggest little word in any language, on any world.

After dinner, the dueling matches began.

It seemed that for fennics, entertainment wasn't watching TV or playing cards but playing at combat. Two would pair off, draw weapons—swords, daggers, spears, whatever—and fight to first blood. Lots of them had scars on their faces that would do justice to Heidelberg. Each slice would bring roars of laughter from the fennics—and bring a silent slave onto the scene with a medical kit.

"Our turn," said Scud, and I nearly jumped out of my skin.

Chapter 23

To no one's surprise, especially mine, I was no match for Scud. I thrusted, he parried, and that snarl that passed for a stupid grin never left his pyramidal face. While I was wearing myself out, the fennic was merely warming himself up. I'd only had a month's worth of instruction; he'd been doing this all his life. It was a game of cat and mouse, but I was the mouse and the cat was a rat.

Finally, the fennic erupted in a flurry of action, driving me back, as his fellows cheered and laughed their approval. I tripped over my big feet and fell flat on my back. Scud stood over me and pointed the tip of his blade at my face, moving it back and forth, up and down, as if trying to decide which part of me to lob off . . . first. He drew his lips back, and a few strands of stinking saliva spilled onto my cheek.

Toward the end of my recruit training at Parris Island, our platoon was paired against another for hand-to-hand combat with pugil sticks—think giant Q-tips with sandbags on the ends to simulate rifles with fixed bayonets. We had been outfitted with helmets, along with padded gloves and briefs. My opponent and I fought hard, but neither of us connected with any serious blows. Our platoon mates cheered us on while our DIs screamed all manner of threats against the one who would eventually lose. At one point, we were face-to-face, our sticks pressed against each other, and the other guy whispered, "Whassa matter, swee' pea, afraid to hit me?"

I saw a veil of red before my eyes and blindly abandoned myself to rage. Screaming and assuming my "killer face," I drove my pugil stick solidly up into his groin. His eyes bugged, his jaw fell, his guard dropped just enough, and I let go a swing to the side of his head followed by a swipe to the other side. Back and forth his head snapped as I slammed first one end of the pugil stick and then the other against his helmet. My roar rasped at my throat. The drill instructor blew his whistle, signaling an end to the match. But it meant nothing to me.

Suddenly I was flat on the ground, yanked down by my senior DI, Staff Sergeant Bellows. "You stupid pissant!" he screamed in a voice that came not from his mouth but blew out of his gut. He straddled me and bent way forward, his breath foul from all those stogies he smoked. "One blow to the head is enough to kill your enemy! One! While you're grandstanding with that turd, some other turd could be comin' up behind you. Then you'd be the next one dead, dumbass! Your buddies would have to come back and brave enemy fire to carry out your sorry butt. Do you want to endanger your fellow Marines, private? Do you?" Before I could reply, he continued his rant: "Or, someone else could be sneakin' up behind one of your own fire team members and you wouldn't even know it! Because you'd be thumping on someone who's already dead! That would be your fault, too, private! Do you want to be responsible for getting one of your fellow Marines killed? Do you? Do you? Answer me, you mangy maggot!"

"No, sir!" I shouted from the ground.

"Then get up, Numbnuts, and give your gear to the next recruit! Now!"

Now . . . the fennic called Scud stood over me, as if he too were taunting, "Whassa matter, swee' pea, afraid to hit me?"

The red veil fell over my eyes. I roared—and hurled my sword at Scud's face.

Uh-oh.

A hush fell over the others, the veil fell from my eyes, and I saw more red—blossoming from a line scored across the fennic's furry cheek.

The others rushed me, but Scud motioned them back. He actually helped me up as a slave came forward to dress his wound. "Return his sword," he commanded, and another slave retrieved it and presented it to me, his eyes downcast. I wanted to weep for him.

"A lesson!" Scud shouted to any and all. "Never let your guard down until the enemy is dead. The offworlder has earned our hospitality." He turned and looked away from me toward the others. "Learn!"

Later, I was ushered to a room off the main corridor, with the admonition that a guard would be placed at the main entrance to the cavern in case I impetuously decided to vacate the premises. At least I'd been allowed to keep my parachute and sword. There was no door to my chamber, no bed, not even a wooden pallet to lie on.

Wall sconces cast flickering light from the hallway, and I lay down on the floor with my head on the parachute pack. I knew I wouldn't get much sleep, but I did have to try. Who knew what tomorrow would bring?

My eyes closed and my thoughts wandered to rodents I'd known. This wasn't Disneyworld, and I was no Mouseketeer. On my Earth, rats were either scourged as plague-carriers or, in labs, served science. Here, on Alter Earth, people served the rats. Further, I noted with a certain sense of irony, their language used contractions. Linguistically speaking, I was more closely related to rats than I was to my own species. What a comforting thought.

Sleep, Walker, my mind said. *Sleep.*

Then another voice said something else, barely above a whisper. "There you are."

Startled, I jumped up to see Sandrine standing in the doorway.

Chapter 24

"We must leave," she said, breathing heavily. "Now." She had my sheath knife in her hand, the once bright blade dark in the flickering light. "Fortunately, the guard was facing inside the cave and did not see me approach." She handed me the knife. "He will stand no more guard duty, ever." She looked over her shoulder at the opening to my chamber. "Now let us go."

I took the knife and sheathed it against my calf. "Sandrine—"

"No time for talk," she insisted. "I overheard the fennics as I passed an inner chamber. They said they were going to keep you and use you for breeding stock, whatever that means."

"Damn. What it means is, they have slaves. Human slaves."

My words hit her like a slap across the face. She opened her mouth as if to say something, then thought better of it. "Later we can talk. Now we go."

"Just a sec." I had her strap on my sword, then I put my parachute pack on and tightened the buckles so they wouldn't clink. Sandrine looked at me nervously, clenching and unclenching her fists. The pack had been in the plane's luggage compartment until now; she'd never noticed it. "Ready," I whispered, and we turned toward the doorway.

"Ready for what?" asked Scud.

"Oh, no," moaned Sandrine. "I was so careful to be quiet."

"So you have an accomplice?" asked the fennic. "How cute. And obviously not an offworlder like your-

self." Five crude stitches held his cheek closed where
my sword had sliced it.

Sandrine made to draw the sword, but then Ulm
and three other fennics emerged to stand behind
Scud, and we knew it was hopeless.

"Why would you want to leave us so soon?" asked
Scud. "After we've been so kind to you? No answer?
Very well, let's go." The fennics grabbed us and followed their chief to the cave opening. The full moon
illuminated a splash of blood on the terrace, but it
drew no expressions of regret or anger from the fennics; more like amusement, in fact. Scud pointed out
at the emptiness before us. "There's the only way out."
Then he said to his comrades, as if we weren't there,
"I'm thinking that maybe I've changed my mind about
the offworlder."

"How so?" asked Ulm.

"How do we know an offworlder would be able to
make offspring with the females? He looks like a human, but I'm convinced he's not one of them. There are
legends we've all heard . . . but enough. Now, the new-
comer, the female, that's a different matter. She looks
healthy. She could shoot out more brats to replace
the ones the gorgons take. I'm thinking we should
send her to the slave pens and toss him." Something
seemed to amuse him. "See if he can go to sleep and
return to his own world before he hits the bottom." He
laughed, and the others joined him.

Sandrine spat at Scud. "I would kill myself before
I submitted to you."

"You would? We'll see now, won't we?"

"Now wait a minute, fellas," I said. "Look, I really
think I'm the one you should keep alive. Forget this
female, I know her. And I know her dirty little secret.
She's barren. That's right, guys, she can't conceive.
Dry as the desert dust down there. She won't give you
any slave babies. Now . . . it's true you could keep her
as a slave, but again, I know her. She'll eat your food,
but she won't do your work. Look at her. She's strong
enough to make other slaves do her work for her. Let

me tell you, this female is one lazy sow. You do have sows here on this world, don't you?"

Sandrine looked at me as if I were her world's version of Benedict Arnold. Her mouth opened and closed, but no words came out.

"On the other hand, look at me. I'm strong, and I'm healthy, like her, but I'm definitely not lazy. I may not be genetically compatible with your slave women, but you know, I'll give it my best shot." I Groucho'ed my eyebrows. "And if it doesn't work out, hey, you'll still have me as a slave. I might not be happy, but at least I'd be alive. Anything's better than being a grease spot on the desert down there. Man, I am *so* afraid of heights. I look over the edge of a building or a cliff and I just want to puke."

The fennics relaxed their hold on us and began to slip into superiority complex mode.

"I mean, if you were determined to toss one of us off this cliff, I'd do anything you wanted to make sure it wasn't me. Anything." Some of the fennics cocked their heads, like a dog that doesn't quite understand. "That's right. I'd do it myself if need be."

"You would kill her to save yourself?" asked Scud.

"Wouldn't you? Hey, look out for Number One." I stared into his tiny black eyes and squinted my baby blues. "Why don't you test me?"

Sandrine snarled at me. "You . . . betrayer!"

"You see? It's all about her."

Scud looked from one of us to the other. He nodded to the others and they released us.

Sandrine backed to the edge of the cliff, staring daggers at me as I advanced toward her. "No hard feelings, babe," I said. "Just gonna toss you into the briar patch is all."

Then I lunged at Sandrine and hit her hard, flat-handed, smack against her shoulders. She flew back over the ledge and disappeared. I turned to the fennics. "See?" Then I jumped after her.

Chapter 25

I had pushed hard enough, I hoped, to keep Sandrine clear of the nearly vertical cliff face. The moonlight revealed her below me, arms and legs thrashing as if seeking some invisible source of support, something she could grasp onto to keep her away from the ground.

I immediately assumed the delta freefall position, arms back like the wings of a fighter plane, and plummeted forward, head low, until I was nearly level with her; then I transitioned into frog position to slow down.

Advanced freefall entails treating your body as if it were an airplane. You can make it go forward, backward, from side to side, even do loops, rolls, and other aerobatics. You can truly fly your body like a plane—in any direction, that is, but up. You then graduate to what's called relative work, when you team up to do simple things like pass a baton back and forth, then learn more intricate maneuvers like the star formation, where you hold hands with as many other jumpers as can fit in the plane and form a circle. Your extended legs form the points of the star. It's exhilarating.

Fifty seconds, I thought as I fell; *thirty-five until I have to pull.* Sandrine was still thrashing about, some ten feet horizontally from me. "Stop moving!" I shouted. "Spread your arms and legs! Now!" She turned her head and seemed to notice me for the first time. Her mouth began to form words, but I shouted "Now!" again, as if I were her drill instructor, and she held still. *Good girl,* I thought as I tilted my feet up and flew toward her.

We collided more than hooked up, but at least we were together. I flipped her back to the earth and positioned myself above her. "Hold on!" I shouted, and she wrapped her arms and legs around me as I steered us away from the cliff.

"Put your arms between my back and the pack!" I shouted in her ear as the rushing air snapped her hair around her face like tiny whips. She struggled to do it, but the pack was tight to my body, as it properly should have been—for any occasion but this one. "Hurry!"

As I mentally ticked off the seconds, I felt Sandrine's fingers finally slide firmly beneath the pack and lock against my spine. Her legs were already hooked around my butt. "Hold on tight, you're going to feel a jerk!" I shouted, thinking, *I'm the jerk for having gotten us into this mess. If only I'd not stopped for those stupid strawberries.*

There was that *if* again.

My right hand found the main chute's D-ring and pulled, hard. I could feel the pilot chute deploy from the pack and hear the main canopy flutter free as my hand slid through the D-ring and both arms wrapped themselves around Sandrine's waist, holding her tightly against me.

"Oof!" The chute wasn't used to supporting an extra hundred and twenty pounds or so, but at least we were upright, stable, and hanging safely beneath a beautiful sailwing canopy that shone a patriotic red, white, and blue in the yellow moonlight.

Sandrine held onto me, mouth agape, eyes wide as saucers, and stared at my grinning mug. "Sacred excrement!" she shouted.

And then we thumped in.

Without the luxury of a rigging table, I was still able to give the chute a decent field pack with Sandrine's help. Then we took a moment to regroup. I looked around and saw the jellied body of a fennic lying nearby. His head had struck a rock, and the resulting splatter looked like my sainted mother's killer chili.

"Your handiwork, I presume," I said.

"I had to cut through his windpipe to silence a scream. It was not pleasant. But now, knowing that they keep my people as slaves . . ."

"And food," I added.

"I would like to cut through the windpipes of all of them." She looked at the body. "I thought, when you pushed me, that I would end up like that."

"Sorry I didn't have time to explain. Come on, let's get walking."

We turned to the west, where Oreste had said the cliff and the ground nearly converged at a small waterfall. Once there, I figured we could scale the slope and double back to the plane. It seemed to be our best option.

As we set out, Sandrine asked me about my *fall-restraining device,* and I told her what I knew of the history of skydiving, from the father of the sport, Jacques Istel, to the evolution of the modern sailwing. She was fascinated. "Now that I have done it once, I would like to try it again."

"The second time's usually scarier than the first," I said. "Second time, you're more aware of what you're doing."

"I do not think I could be more frightened than I was . . . or angrier at you for your cowardly betrayal."

"I hope I'm forgiven for that. And you owe me an explanation too. Like, how come you never told me that nature over here let spiders and rats evolve into human form? I mean, letting them speak and think and all?"

"You mean, that is not the way in your world? Are you telling me that only one species is sentient, your own?"

"Yes. That is, I think so. Someone once wrote that dolphins are far superior."

"I apologize, Aldenwalker. When my father and I mentioned the others, the ones responsible for the great cataclysm, we assumed you knew it would be . . . nonhumans. You seemed to accept the existence of gorgons without question."

"Yeah, well, vampires are part of my own world too, but where I come from they're only stories, and thank you for not reminding me that I'm no longer where I come from."

"You are welcome."

We walked on in the moonlight, through a desert that reminded me of the American Southwest more than, say, the Sahara. Cacti and shrubs dotted the landscape, and I remembered reading somewhere that the flesh of the barrel cactus could provide moisture enough to quench a person's thirst. I cut one up and we tried it. The taste was tart enough to make us pucker, but we did get some moisture out of it. And we knew it would help assuage hunger pangs later.

As dawn broke, we gave in to our need for sleep. We found a shallow cave at the base of the escarpment and ducked inside for the shade. I took off the chute and insisted Sandrine use it as a pillow. We sat with our backs to the cave wall, Sandrine to my left.

"What is that silver band around your finger?" she asked, her voice soft.

"It's a wedding ring," I said and explained the whole marriage thing.

"That seems strange," she said, and when I asked why she continued: "Why on your world do lovers need a third party to pronounce them pledged? How could some stranger know their hearts better than they know themselves?"

"You're right, I suppose. There's more to it than that, though . . . but what do you do here?"

"When . . . when Ander and I knew we were mates, we simply pledged our lives to each other. No one stood before us to pronounce us mated, and no guests were in attendance. It was a private matter. Intimate."

"Something to be said for that, I suppose."

"May I ask you a question, Aldenwalker?"

"Of course."

"It might be too private or painful for you to share."

"Only one way to find out, isn't there?"

She took a deep breath and turned her face toward mine. "How did your consort die?"

Chapter 26

Lynda Murray had always been a daredevil. As a six-year-old, she figured out how Superman flew and tested her theory by tying a dish towel around her neck for a cape and sliding down the porch rail, head first, pulling at the air with her hands and kicking at it with her feet. *As long as I keep pulling and pushing,* she believed, *I'll be able to fly too.* She wondered why no one else had ever figured it out before now.

When she picked herself up from the grass and wiped the blood from her chin where it had met a hidden rock, she figured it might be time to modify her theory. The scar from that incident remained with her, but the lesson didn't.

As a teenager, she *borrowed* a friend's motorcycle when he wasn't looking; and that resulted in another scar, this one on her leg, when she tumbled while making a too-sharp turn.

In college, she tried bungee jumping from a bridge. But she didn't take into account the recent heavy rains that had raised the water level of the river below, and when her head hit the water, the impact nearly knocked her out. When she sprung back, her lungs were full of water. Fortunately, thanks to gravity, the water drained out quickly.

Lynda graduated college with a degree in journalism and wrote of her adventures and misadventures for her local paper. The Baltimore *Sun* took note and hired her away as a reporter and columnist. She wrote a weekly feature that appeared every Sunday entitled "Girls Do It," and—thanks to the photographs that always accompanied each story—as many men as women formed her readership. Lynda's IQ was matched only by her high BQ: beauty quotient.

Despite the obvious slant of her column's title, Lynda's articles were decidedly unsexy. Each week she would participate in an out-of-the-mainstream activity and commit the experience to a few thousand well-chosen words. As a stand-up comic she fell flat, but her readers admired her courage nevertheless. As a novice nightclub singer, it was her notes that fell flat. She did much better as a circus clown, and the little girls loved the glamour-clown make-up she herself had designed. She spent a few days with a sailboat racing crew on the Chesapeake Bay and found it—no disrespect intended, she wrote—incredibly boring.

Lynda needed adrenaline, and when she learned of a new skydiving center down on the Delmarva Peninsula, she immediately called to make an appointment for her first jump.

Her instruction took an entire morning, during which she squirmed restlessly through all the safety procedures her instructor, a guy with the unusual name of Alden, insisted she learn. She had already signed the I-won't-sue-you-if-I-die waiver; could she just get into the plane and go? But no, she had to learn all about the gear—the piggyback parachute pack, which carried both the main chute and the reserve in one neat package; aerodynamic theory—arch and spread position, I've got it already; proper way to exit the aircraft and land—so can we get started, please?

I swear, Lynda thought, *this guy Alden must walk around with a broomstick up his butt.* Did he ever loosen up? Safety, safety, safety, the need for redundancy (you can say that again). I'll bet he double-knots his shoelaces and does a thirty-minute car inspection before driving down the street for a quart of milk. *Listen,* she wanted to tell him, *you're the one going to do the work. I'm just going to be attached to your harness, going along for the ride.*

She still wanted to be Superman.

Finally, they crawled into the plane. The air-to-air videographer, part of the training package, had swapped his camcorder for a helmet-mounted still camera and was waiting for them in the rear-facing jump seat next to the pilot. There were no other seats, just padding on the floor and along the interior bulkhead.

At thirteen thousand feet, Alden hooked his harness to Lynda's. They would exit and fall face down, his belly against her back. When they were ready, Alden nodded to the photographer, who nodded to the pilot, who pulled the throttle back to slow the plane down for their exit. The photographer climbed out and positioned himself in front of the wing strut as the others took their position on the step behind it. With another nod, the photographer dropped away, followed immediately by Alden and Lynda.

She was surprised she felt no sensation of falling, no more than when she dived from a board into a pool. In fact, her body seemed to settle on the air as if it were on water, and the pressure of the air beneath her seemed to hold her up, not let her down. There was no indication of the ground's rushing up to meet her.

The photographer clicked away, nearly filling the memory card before they reached the halfway mark in their freefall. In every picture, Lynda wore a smile that said *I've found the ultimate thrill. This is mine, this is my life.* What she would notice later was that in the photos Alden was grinning just as broadly as she. She decided she liked his smile.

Lynda watched the altimeter and stopwatch attached to her instructor's wrist wind down (there's that redundancy again), and when the altimeter needle reached the red pie-shaped wedge Alden popped the chute. Within seconds, they were swinging under the canopy, enjoying the sudden silence, watching the photographer descend beneath them under his own chute.

"Want to steer?" asked Alden, and he handed her the toggles. Lynda remembered the first time her dad had allowed her to work the steering wheel of the family car at thirteen, and the thrill she'd had controlling its direction as it *hurtled* along the country road at thirty-five miles per hour. That was nothing. This was amazing.

After they'd landed and shed their harnesses, Lynda turned to Alden and in her glee planted a big wet kiss on his lips. Then she pulled away, apologizing that she'd gotten carried away there.

"Don't apologize," he commanded, and kissed her back, hard and long.

Alden had said a small-scale wedding officiated by a justice of the peace would suit him just fine, but Lynda had other plans. "Don Wilson's a minister," she said. "He can marry us in freefall. Wouldn't that be great? Something to tell our kids about?"

Alden gave in, as he always did, but he still insisted on proper safety protocols. They would be married inside the plane. Don could pronounce them man and wife as they jumped. They would reach terminal velocity, do a few coordinated aerobatics, then hold hands facing each other until it was time to pull. And she was *not* to prime her pins.

The typical parachute pack is held shut by steel pins threaded through locking cones. The pins are fastened to the ripcord cable, which in turn is threaded through a gooseneck housing that goes over the jumper's shoulder and is attached at the other end to a steel handle called a D-ring. To open the pack, the jumper grabs the D-ring and pulls, extending his arm fully to ensure the cord is free. After the chute opens, he slips the D-ring over his wrist as he reaches for the steering toggles.

Lynda didn't like having the ripcord wire flapping about in the wind before the chute opened. So she developed the habit of packing her chute with the pins only half inserted through the locking cones. That way, she could just give a tiny tug on the D-ring and let go, leaving the ripcord inside the gooseneck during opening and descent.

This was called priming one's pins. To Lynda, it was called finesse. To Alden, it was called stupid.

Lynda gave in and promised her fiancé she wouldn't prime her pins. She'd lied. And Alden, the nervous groom, missed seeing it.

The jump went according to plan. Don—with *The Rev* stenciled on the front of his helmet and a camcorder attached to the side recording everything—had them exchange their vows and their rings while the plane climbed to jump altitude. As they left the aircraft, he pronounced them husband and wife and fell alongside them as they somersaulted, played ring around the rosy, and finally linked hands facing each other.

Lynda looked at her wrist instruments and knew in three seconds they would have to pull. Instead of breaking away, she drew Alden closer. She laughed as he shook his head no and pulled his face to hers for their wedding kiss. With her mouth fast to his, his resistance took the form of urgent grunts. Finally he shoved her away and pulled his ripcord. Don was already under his canopy high above them.

Lynda was in heaven. The wind whistled through her helmet, her wedding song. Okay, she thought, time to pop. She gave a little tug and waited for the opening shock. It didn't come. She looked back and saw the pilot chute trying bravely to pull the main free. She tugged again, and nothing. Unknown to her, one of her pins had not pulled completely free from its locking cone, and the pressure of the chute's attempt to pull up into the airstream had bent the pin and locked it into place.

She pulled and pulled, losing all aerodynamics and rolling over, back to earth. She couldn't see the ground approach, but from somewhere far away she thought she might have heard someone shouting her name.

Lynda panicked. She was too close and she knew it. Her other hand reached for the D-ring of the emergency chute and yanked, hard. The ripcord flew free, and her body turned face to earth as the chute deployed.

That's when she saw the faces of the guests and heard their screams. Too close and too loud. It was the last thing she saw, the last thing she heard. She didn't even have time to form a final thought: *Alden, I'm so sorry.*

Chapter 27

Telling the story to Sandrine, the first time I'd told it to anyone, proved cathartic. And she proved empathetic. We truly did seem bound by our mutual loss. We dozed at least half the day away inside the cave. Prudence told me we should spell each other on guard duty, but I was too tired to listen to prudence, and Sandrine didn't seem too worried, either. The fennics probably figured I'd chosen a murder-suicide as the better alternative to what life with them offered us. They didn't know what was in my pack and obviously had no idea what a parachute even was. In other words, we felt safe from pursuit. Unless . . .

Unless they had looked over the edge after us, saw a red, white, and blue speck float to the ground under the moonlight, and had more than two miles' worth of rappelling line at their disposal. As I said: safe. From the fennics, anyway.

Late in the afternoon, we heard a noise from deeper inside the cave. Standing, we saw something slither out and heard a dry, ominous rattle.

The sidewinder was as thick as my thigh, its body in perfect proportion. In other words, huge. And judging by the way it reared up to stare me in the eyes, it was gauging me a perfect fit for its gullet.

"Give me the sword, slowly," I said.

"I can—"

"Just please, give me the sword. You get the next one. And make it slow and easy, no sudden moves."

Sandrine slipped the pommel of the sword into my hand and I edged to the side, away from her. "Don't make a sound," I cautioned.

"Aldenwalker, ophidians are deaf."

"But they can feel vibrations, which is what I'm making now to keep his attention on me. See how his precious little wedge-shaped head is tracking my movements?"

Let's see, I thought, trying to remember facts from my biology classes. *Cold-blooded. Cave is cooler than the desert during the day, warmer during the cold desert night. Rattler holes up, comes out in the afternoon to warm up, maybe grab a bite to eat. Might be a little sluggish until the sun hits him and warms him up. Please,* I prayed, *be sluggish.*

The snake's head danced some ten feet from mine, just beyond my reach. It opened its mouth and I saw its fangs, drops of venom forming at their tips. If this thing bit my arm, the fangs would go right through and out the other side. I tensed my grip on the sword. This would be a one-shot deal. I stopped breathing, waited . . .

And saw a rock bounce off the snake's head. As it spun to face Sandrine, I leaped forward and swung the sword as hard as I could. It bit into the snake's neck with a *chunk*—and found its way between two vertebrae, shearing through. The head fell to the ground between Sandrine and me, still attached to its writhing body by a strip of skin. Body and head banged against the cave wall as Sandrine and I bolted out of the way. Blood sprayed from the trunk, spattering us with gore as we retreated onto the desert sand.

"You grow them big here," I said as we watched the snake's death throes lessen and finally stop altogether.

"And you look a mess," she said, then laughed. I could see the tension melt away from her, and I laughed, too.

"What a team," I said, "what a team."

With the snake dead, we returned to the cave. I picked up my parachute pack, and Sandrine picked up the denuded barrel cactus. She was ready to leave, but I stopped her. "Will you give me a hand here?" I asked.

"Aldenwalker," Sandrine said, puzzled, "there are many things I would be happy to give you, but my body parts are not among them."

I stared at her for a second, to make sure she wasn't joking. "You really do need some idioms here," I said. "I mean, lend me a hand; no, I mean give me some help. With your hands. See?"

She shook her head. "What is it you would like me to *give you a hand* with?"

I stared at the snake and the flesh of the barrel cactus and said, "Sandrine, have you ever heard of sushi?"

I'd never been a fan of raw anything, so what we ate would never rank high on my list of favorites; but eat it we did, until we couldn't force any more down. And no, it didn't taste like chicken.

We began walking again, toward the setting sun. Sandrine asked about my parents and I told her both had died prematurely: my father from three packs a day, my mother from runaway diabetes. Sandrine couldn't understand why someone would deliberately suck hot smoke into his body, and she didn't quite get it when I told her that it involved some kind of chemically-induced euphoria.

"But it is poison," she protested. "That is what you said. Do the others not know that?"

"They know it full well."

"Yours must be a suicidal race."

"Not all of us. And those who do pick up the addiction don't see themselves as suicidal either. There are more efficient ways to kill yourself than by playing slow-motion Russian roulette." She questioned the term. "Never mind."

"And what is this dia . . ."

"Diabetes." I told her of the disease and its effects. "My mother and father died the same year. She went first. But not before she developed gangrene in one leg, and it had to come off."

"That is sad."

"Yes. It is. But something weird happened to her when she was on the operating table. During one of my visits she told me about it. Said she couldn't tell my dad, he would've said she was hallucinating. But she knew I was more open-minded than my dad, and she had to share the experience with someone."

"What was it?"

"I remember her words almost exactly. She said, 'The strangest thing happened. I died. That's right, dear, I died. My spirit left my body and floated above me. I saw myself under the anesthetic and saw the doctor operating on my leg. He was wearing a green T-shirt under his scrubs, like yours when you were in the Marines, and his scrubs were green too, but a different shade, lighter. He had a blue hairnet-type cap tied on his head. He was sweating, and he would scold the nurse if she wasn't right there to mop his brow. A young nursing student was in the operating room, and when she heard the sound of the bone saw cutting through my leg, she fainted. Poor child fell forward and bloodied her nose when she hit the floor.' Now, that's what my mother told me. She also said she was told by someone *over there* to come back to tell me about this; that she had seen the afterlife, and that she wasn't afraid anymore to die. Which she did, peacefully, two months later. What do you think?"

"I think I would have to agree with your father. She was hallucinating."

"I'd have believed that, too, if it weren't for two things."

"What?"

"First, I checked with the surgeon. Everything my mother reported to me happened exactly as she said."

"Truly? That is strange."

"Wait, it gets better. See, the disease, the diabetes, had stolen my mother's sight. She'd been totally blind for five years."

106

Chapter 28

They walked on silently, each immersed in thought, as the sun began its descent toward the horizon. Their eyes fell to the ground before them as their shoulders sagged from the heat and the monotony of putting one foot in front of the other. The plan was to walk through the night, when the temperature was cold, and doze the next day, shaded from the sun in a hollow in the cliff face.

Sandrine thought of Aldenwalker's story, of his father's smoke-related suicide (as she thought of it) and his mother's experience in the operating room. She was inclined to think of the event as a drug-induced hallucination, but the detail with which he had described it, and his conviction in the telling, gave it credence. Her partner in this quest was not prone to embellishment. Sarcastic he could be, and some of his verbal expressions—*give me a hand* came to mind— made her smile at their incongruity. But—aside from the quick-thinking trickery he employed against the fennics when he shoved her over the cliff—he was not prone to lying. His integrity, she knew by now, was beyond reproach.

They had been constant companions for a lune, and their relationship had grown from that of strangers to one of shared friendship. Both seemed to be of one mind, and Sandrine wondered if that would extend beyond the completion of their quest—if indeed they were able to remain alive to complete it. The plan had seemed simple when she and her father had conceived it, but perhaps it had been too simple. Their encounter with the fennics had proved they had not considered the need for contingencies, such as weather. Now they were without their airship, they were on foot for who knew how long, and every day they delayed was a day closer to the time when the gorgons would learn to master the bridge. Once they did, no one would be safe. The world would be their feed pen.

Her mind returned to Aldenwalker, or Alden Walker, as he had referred to himself. He had told her once that Walker was a *family* name, which indicated to her that on his world family was an institution of sorts. In her world, families were important too, but family names as such were irrelevant. Everyone in her keep, for example, had but one name and was considered part of the same family.

Aldenwalker would be returning to his family once the mission was successful. But in conversation as they hiked on toward the waterfall he had admitted he had no family left. In truth, he had no family on either world. He was alone, and—as she well knew—being alone could be devastating. Having one's consort snatched suddenly and horribly from one's life brought grief beyond measure.

Would he have reason to return to his own world? Would he want to?

And, Sandrine thought, *what would that mean to me?*

She glanced at Aldenwalker, trudging next to her, his head bowed as if his eyes were boring holes in the earth. How terrified he must have been when he encountered the arachnid queen; and when he was captured by the fennics, neither of whose existence he had even remotely suspected. How infuriated he must have been when he discovered fennics used humans as slaves—and also as food. Did that not give him a vested interest in the affairs of her world?

Until hearing Aldenwalker's story about his mother, Sandrine had never considered the possibility of life's continuing after physical death. If his mother's story were true, then both Ander and her own mother were somehow alive still, albeit in a dimension beyond their ability to bridge. It was interesting to contemplate, and it gave her a sense of comfort that had been missing before.

Her mind returned to Ander, and she wondered if she were being disloyal to his memory by taking note of Aldenwalker's exotic and yet somehow pleasing appearance; his stoic acceptance of the mission that was forced upon him; his bravery in facing his fears in what was for him an alien environment. What would Ander have thought? More importantly, what would he have wanted for her?

Both she and Aldenwalker were bereft of their consorts. Too, he had lost both parents; she had lost one. In some distant . . . afterlife . . . they might all be reunited. Meanwhile, their lives in this dimension continued, and it was imperative to live one life at a time.

Sandrine glanced sideways at Aldenwalker. He was still staring at the ground, bowed forward slightly to balance the weight of his parachute pack. She turned toward the sun, just beginning to turn the sky pink. Something caught her eye above, and her blood froze in her veins. She grabbed his arm and pulled them both to the ground.

"Wha—" he began, but she clamped a hand over his mouth and nodded toward the sky. He turned his head and saw, high above the cliff, what appeared to be six large birds, riding the mountain wave of rising air, their wings still as they glided toward the east.

She took her hand from his mouth and whispered: "*Ampairs.*"

Chapter 29

Well, now I'd seen them. They weren't abstractions anymore. We lay unmoving on the sand, watching them grow smaller in the distance until they were out of sight.

"Doesn't sunlight kill them?" I thought aloud.

"What?"

"Sorry. Forget I said that. So. Those are gorgons. Where do you suppose they're headed?"

"I do not know. I only hope it is not to our keep." Sandrine shuddered.

"Oh. Right." We stood up and brushed ourselves off. If they were in fact headed toward the keep, there was nothing we could do about it anyway. We could only hope they had another destination in mind. "There's a barrel cactus over there," I said. "You hungry?"

Sandrine twisted her mouth. "What do you think? Are you hungry?"

"My stomach thinks my throat's been cut." I slipped out of the parachute pack and let it drop. Taking my knife out of my leg sheath, I sliced off the spines and dug out some of the flesh. When I turned to face Sandrine, I stopped cold. "Sandrine. Don't move. Don't even breathe." She frowned, but complied instantly. That's discipline.

Behind her crawled a gila monster. At least that's what it looked like, Alter Earth version: mottled body, thick tail, and a butt-ugly head with poison between its jaws. As the snake was larger than life, so was this lizard. Its warty body stood at least a foot, maybe more, above the ground. Now I had an idea of what the oversized rattler might see as prey.

The lizard's slimy tongue flicked out and back as it approached Sandrine. Her boots would probably be thick enough to deflect its teeth, but I didn't think it intended to attack her anyway. It was probably searching for a meal, and she was way too big. At least that's what I thought.

Sandrine must have heard the monster's belly dragging across the sand, and she chanced to look down just as its head was next to her boot. Reflexively, she snapped her leg to the side, knocking it away, and then turned to face it. It stared back at her, and if a lizard could manage to look p.o.'ed, well, that's what it did. It opened its mouth and hissed. Its teeth were small, all of the same size, and needle sharp, like those of the bluefish I used to catch as a boy. Or maybe like the piranhas that I'd seen only in pictures.

Sandrine reached down and drew the sword from its sheath, just as the lizard charged. It closed too fast and got inside her guard before she could bring the blade down. It lunged, and its jaws sank into the top of her boot. She shook her leg, but it held on like a pit bull, its stubby legs free of the ground, its fleshy tail swinging back and forth. I could see the poison saliva dripping down Sandrine's boot.

"Some . . . help, please?" she grunted and I snapped out of my temporary paralysis. I rushed over and drove my knife into the monster's side. It let go of Sandrine and thrashed about, trying to bite me as I twisted my blade inside its thick and heavy body.

The thing refused to die. And it was strong. Strong enough to make me wonder if I could hold onto this dervish much longer. But Sandrine distracted it by pointing the sword at its face. It opened its mouth and hissed at her, and she pushed the blade inside . . . and down its throat . . . and all the way out its rear end. It was skewered like a shish kebab. Still it squirmed, and I pulled my knife free as Sandrine tilted the sword's hilt skyward and anchored the blade into the ground. She backed away and watched the animal's death throes with me.

It was dusk now, and we could feel the chill start to creep in. While there was still some light, I gutted the gila monster and filleted it as well as I could. I presented the first piece to Sandrine, atop a slice of moist and tart barrel cactus. I exaggerated my posture and movements as if I were a veddy propah English butler. She wrinkled her nose and said, as if she were a petulant child, "Sushi *again*?"

Although I've never been a smoker, I wished I'd had the foresight to bring a pack of matches with me anyway. Or at least a couple of Boy Scouts to rub together. Cooked lizard might've been endurable, but raw lizard—coupled with the sour taste of cactus—just wouldn't make an epicurean's top ten list. Nevertheless, we forced it down, and our stomachs soon stopped growling. I offered my parachute pack to Sandrine to use as a seat while I stood. Limned by the moonlight, chewing daintily on the gila monster's flesh, she looked downright fetching. Delicate, even. Although I wouldn't have dared tell her that: the way she treated those arachnids who'd tried to mate with her; the way she slit the throat of the fennic guarding the cave entrance; the way she braved the rattlesnake—all that and more took her way out of the debutante's ball category. In my father's day, it was the man who protected his woman, and some of that attitude had naturally rubbed off on me. But that was on my world, and as you-know-who had frequently reminded me, I wasn't on my world anymore.

Sandrine might not have been as physically strong as I, but she was at least as agile if not more so. And as for her courage, well, I'd share a foxhole with her any time.

From somewhere came the thought I might like to share more than a foxhole with her. Then, feeling like a cheating husband, I thought back to Lynda, whom I'd lost because I'd not been protective enough, and with whom as a consequence I would never share my life. I thought of our moments together: making parachute jumps; making plans for home and hearth; making love—and nearly choked when the image of my making love to that . . . creature . . . intruded on my consciousness. How could the arachnid queen, that anthropomorphic spider, reach into my mind and make me see her as Lynda? Would my image of Lynda be tainted forever by the memory of the widow?

"You are quiet, Aldenwalker," said Sandrine as she stood up, her such-as-it-was meal finished.

"I was just thinking."

"About what?"

"About how pretty you look in the moonlight, with that lizard juice dribbling down your chin."

She laughed and tossed the parachute at me, one-handed, before she wiped her mouth on her sleeve.

We continued walking, the moon lighting our way, the shivers a constant companion. I knew deserts got cold at night no matter how hot they were during the day, but I'd never experienced it firsthand. After a few hours, we both admitted that we'd need to rest. We found an indentation in the cliff face and settled in, promising to nap for *just a little while.* We sat side-by-side and drew our knees up, resting against the stone. Our shivering didn't let up, and without a word Sandrine leaned into me. I put my arm around her shoulders and rested my cheek on the top of her head. Her hair was soft and fine, and I found myself wanting to wrap my other arm around her too. But I didn't.

Moments later, Sandrine turned toward me and unselfconsciously wrapped her free arm around my waist, snuggling tight. Her shivering stopped, and she was asleep in seconds. I leaned my head back and gazed at the moon, high in the sky. A silhou-ette passed before it, heading west in the direction of the mountain keep; then another, and another, six all told. Like large birds they were, but this time they weren't gliding, they were flapping their giant wings, and their bodies seemed to be nearly doubled in thickness from before.

There was nothing to be gained by waking Sandrine. I nodded my head forward, closed my eyes, and slept.

I snapped my head up suddenly, opened my eyes, and saw the beginnings of daylight. So much for a little nap. Sandrine still slept across my legs, serene in her slumber. I hated to wake her, but wake her I did, and she fairly leaped to her feet, eager to begin the day's march. As we walked, I told her about seeing the gorgons and speculated that they probably didn't have time to reach Oreste's keep and backtrack between the hours of their going and coming. Of course, that was just speculation, but I said it with more authority than I felt, out of consideration for Sandrine's anxiety.

Two hours or so into our hike I noticed that the air seemed less dry than before. Then something buzzed in my ear, and I swatted at it. A mosquito, and a normal-sized one at that, thank goodness. Water could not be far away. The ground started looking more like dirt than sand, as well, and when we looked up we saw the cliff rose no more than fifty feet above us now. Still vertical, though; we'd have to see if there were rocks we could climb closer to the waterfall that, according to Oreste, had to be up ahead.

Then we saw it, and Sandrine whooped with delight. The fall was no Niagara, another good sign; instead, it was a gentle spill into what looked like a deep pool at its base, before the river meandered away westward toward the sea. We could see the tops of trees poking above the cliff. Paradise, or a reasonable facsimile, was not that far above us.

"We shall be able to wash in the river," said Sandrine, looking up. "I cannot wait."

I thought about washing, the two of us, and the word *clothes* entered my thoughts. What were the rules here concerning communal bathing?

At the edge of the pool, I bent over and splashed water onto my face, cleaning it of the crusted blood from the snake and lizard. Sandrine followed suit. Neither of us drank, figuring the water would be cleaner above, as it ran over the rocks, rather than sitting relatively still here. I adjusted the parachute pack on my back so it wouldn't hang loose as I climbed. Sandrine still wore the sword in its scabbard at her waist.

Before we began our ascent, I found a flat stone and picked it up. "Hey, Sandrine, when I was a kid I used to be a champ at this." She watched, bemused, as I threw it across the pool. It skipped five times before disappearing below the water.

It wasn't the smartest move I'd ever made.

Chapter 30

The cliff had eroded so much here, it was more a pile of rocks and rubble than a vertical escarpment; in other words, an easy climb. "Let's go," I said.

We hadn't climbed more than five feet when Sandrine screamed and a truck slammed into my back, smashing my face against the rocks. My nose crumpled like an accordion and blood gushed both into and out of my mouth. Sandrine shrieked again and held onto me as something began pulling me back toward the water.

Whatever was holding me was not letting go, and it would only be a matter of seconds before I'd have to release my own grip. "Hold fast!" Sandrine commanded, and before I could burble that it was impossible she drew her sword and began chopping at something behind me, again and again. "Die! Die!" she shouted, and chopped and chopped and chopped some more.

Something behind me gave, and we became awash in a geyser of blood. My feet were slipping on the now-scarlet stones, but somehow my fingers held fast, and then the pulling stopped altogether. Something splashed into the water behind me. Something big.

I spit blood, and my tongue probed a mouthful of loose teeth. My nose was in agony. I turned to where Sandrine was holding onto me and saw her bathed in blood too, as if she had stepped out of a certain Stephen King movie. I didn't have that much blood in my whole body; it couldn't all have been mine. But still . . .

She shook the blood out of her eyes and held me steady. "You look terrible," she gasped, as if I needed reminding, and as if she looked any better. "I think I can fix it, once we are at the top. Can you climb, Aldenwalker?"

I spit out more blood. "What do you mean, *think*?" I sputtered.

Sandrine took the lead and half carried me up the rocks to the top—I must have been heavier than I thought—where we found a sprawling meadow bordering the shallow river. She released my pack and it fell to the ground with a squishy sound that I didn't want to investigate just then. "To the river," she directed, holding my arm around her shoulder and sitting me down on the bank with my feet in the icy water. She looked at my face and shook her head sadly. "This will hurt, Aldenwalker, but it is better to do it now than later." And without further ceremony, she grabbed my nose and yanked it straight.

"Yow! You—" She was right, it did hurt. Man, did it hurt. Tears leaped from my eyes to mingle with the blood on my face. "Your nose was pressed flat to the side," Sandrine said apologetically. "It looks almost normal now." She continued to examine her handiwork and appeared satisfied. "Now we must wash you." She scooped water from the river and gingerly rinsed my face. Blood continued to flow from my nose. "Tilt your head back," she said.

"Just tie a tourniquet around my neck."

"Shhh. Be still."

Sandrine pinched my nostrils—I held back a moan—and eventually the bleeding slowed to a trickle. When it had stopped, she pointed behind me to my pack—and the shiny pink bulb that was attached to it. It looked familiar, somehow. Too big, too bloated, but disturbingly familiar.

When I was a kid, my dad would sometimes take me fishing in the Chesapeake Bay for winter flounder, and our bait was always bloodworms. They have whiplike little legs like millipedes and normally hide in sea grass. When one gets hungry, it actually propels its stomach out of its mouth at its prey. The stomach has four hooks on it, which capture the prey and drag it back into the worm's body, where it's digested. Alive. When you cut up one of these critters to put it on the fishhook, the stomach shoots out and the worm's body spurts blood; hence the name.

The bloodworms I had handled were no longer than three inches. I had no idea how long this one was, but the stomach alone covered my whole parachute pack. Had I not been wearing it, the wickedly-curved hooks would've sunk into my body.

"Something else you forgot to tell me about?" I slurred, spitting more blood.

"I did not know. I had never heard of such a thing." Obviously, there were some serious gaps in Sandrine's education.

Suddenly I felt lightheaded. Whatever blood I had left was draining from my head. "Sandrine, I think I'm going to faint now." And I did.

When I came to, it was late afternoon, my parachute pack was free of the bloodworm's stomach, and I was lying stark naked where I'd fallen. My battered jumpsuit and skivvies were drying on a tree limb, and Sandrine was sitting on a nearby rock. Smiling at me. Fully clothed in her freshly washed and dried coveralls.

"You have me at a disadvantage," I said.

"I do," she replied. "It is good you cannot see your face; it is one big bruise." She walked over and held out her hand. "I found some strawberries."

I groaned. "Strawberries are what started this whole mess. But I'm starving. Thanks."

After I'd dressed and gummed the berries—my teeth were still loose, but at least they were all there— she told me after we backtracked and recovered the plane we'd have to fly to the village of River's Reach before heading to the gorgons' lair. I asked why.

"Years ago, well before I was born, fennics raided River's Reach. Understand, weapons as such were unknown in the village at the time; up until then, there had been no need for them. Fennics had not been seen or heard from in ages; some people considered them merely a tale told around a campfire to frighten little children. As it happened, they were definitely not such tales. A cadre of them invaded, killed any who opposed them, drove many more into hiding in the forest, and marched away with scores of prisoners. A militia of sorts formed up, made makeshift weapons of their farming and harvesting tools, and followed them. Neither they nor the prisoners were ever seen again. But a later group found chewed bones scattered along the trail, and they abandoned hope of rescuing the prisoners, assuming they had all been eaten. Now there stands a wall around the village, with guards who carry swords and knives on their persons. But the fennics, thankfully, have not returned."

"They don't need to," I surmised. "They probably have all the slaves they need. And, they probably ate one prisoner and left the bones in plain sight to discourage further pursuit."

"Exactly. But the villagers do not know their people—or, more likely, their people's descendants—still live. That is why we must tell them now."

"You mean, instead of later. Because . . . for us, there may not be a later."

She chose not to respond to the *later* remark. "They need to know, and they need to form an army to free the prisoners. And they need us to tell them where the fennics live."

"Okay, let's do it."

"Aldenwalker." She shook her head, either perplexed or frustrated; more likely, both.

"What?"

"What is this *okay?*"

"Oops." I tried to explain, ending with, "So you can say *okay* when you are satisfied or agree with someone's plan. Or when you want to simply say *yes*. Or if all is correct, and everything is right with the world. Are you . . . okay with that?"

She appeared to think about it. "A multi-purpose word. Understood."

"I give up."

"That means surrender, does it not?"

"You're playing with me, right? You are playing with me. I caught a little twinkle in your eye there, don't deny it."

She didn't answer.

We piled up leaves and brush to serve as a mattress and spread the parachute over them. "I think we should take turns standing guard," I said. "I don't know if anything is out there that could be a danger to us, do you?" She shook her head. "I've slept, so I'll take first watch. I'll wake you up when I get tired. Okay with you?"

"I am satisfied with that. Thank you, Aldenwalker."

I touched my tender nose. "No, thank you—I think."

As the sun set, we watched a family of unicorns—stallion, mare, and colt—emerge from the forest about a tenth of a mile away and begin cropping the grass. Sandrine and I looked from each other to the unicorns—the little one's horn looked like a velvet-covered finger—and thought our private thoughts.

As first watch, I stayed awake for at least half the night, walking in circles around the makeshift bed, checking the meadow or the woods beyond for any movement of the sinister variety, and looking at Sandrine as she slept the sleep of the just. When I woke her, she was up instantly, ready to take her post. After surrendering my sword to her, I stretched out on my side, lay my bruised and still-hurting head against my outstretched arm, and immediately fell asleep.

When I awoke the sun was high, birds were singing, and Sandrine was sound asleep beside me, one arm draped over my waist.

Chapter 31

We breakfasted on more strawberries and fresh cool river water, and as I prepared to field-pack the parachute, the sky clouded over and a gentle rain began to fall.

"We should rest today," Sandrine said. "You need to build up your strength. We can take shelter beneath your canopy."

"What? You think I'm too weak to travel? Because of old Moby Worm back there? You have a lot to learn, young lady." Then my knees kind of wobbled and I lowered myself to the ground. "I hate it when you're right."

She chuckled and sat down next to me, pulling the canopy over us. Her breath smelled like strawberries; I wondered how that worked. If I don't brush after every meal, my own breath is enough to stop a charging rhino. We sat shoulder-to-shoulder, and it felt pretty good, considering.

"Yellow is beginning to mix with the blue and the black on your face," Sandrine said.

"Don't touch it," I cautioned, as her fingers moved toward my nose. "Please?"

Her smile was soft and so was her touch. "Be easy. I only want to—Aldenwalker, what is a lot? You said I have a lot to learn. Does *a lot* mean *much*?"

"You're getting it," I said. Then, "Changing the subject, you heard the fennic chief, Scud, mention making you a breeder to replace the slaves the gorgons take. What do you suppose is the connection between them?"

"Whatever it is, it cannot be good."

"I think I can guess."

"I would not want to. I just would not want to."

"All this," I thought out loud. "It's a crazy world you live in, Sandrine. Magic pixie dust for fuel, human—make that humanoid—vampires, spiders, rats, and who knows what else? Giant snakes and lizards, and bloodworms, oh my? Holy cow, I just had a thought—what would that bloodworm eat? It's enough to make my hair hurt."

Sandrine was about to smooth back my hair, but hesitated. "Your hair hurts? But hair is dead."

I laughed. "Just another expression."

"Like holy cows? Do they make the sacred excrement?" We both laughed now. "Honestly, Aldenwalker, how will I ever learn the peculiarities of your language?"

"Why would you need to?"

Oh no. Open mouth, insert foot.

Her hand, which was level with my cheek, stopped in midair. Her smile disappeared.

Great, you flaming idiot, I thought. *Why didn't you just flip her the bird right then and there to really seal the deal? Except she wouldn't know what that meant either.*

"Sandrine, what I meant was—"

She brought her hand to her lap and stared straight out at the rain. "I know what you meant. You are right. Why would I need to?"

We sat in silence, listening to the rain, feeling it soak through the parachute, getting wet. We still sat shoulder-to-shoulder—but hers had grown cold.

The rain ended finally, and we draped the parachute across some nearby bushes to let the air circulate and dry it out. Sandrine's facial expression remained devoid of emotion, whereas mine must have revealed to her the unspoken apology for my tactless remark. Something had definitely been developing between us over the past several weeks; friendship at first, but once on the mission, with its adventure and attendant dangers, and our respect for and dependence upon each other, I began feeling an attraction that went beyond friendship. Thinking back to that night when she'd slept cuddled next to me, I realized that I really liked having her with me.

Had Sandrine been feeling something for me, something more than platonic? Had she accepted her consort's death and finished grieving? Come to think of it, had I? And if the answer to all those questions was yes, what then? In the old days, some of my former Marine Corps buddies might've suggested that, were she willing, I simply *roll her over in the clover* and let what happened afterward . . . just happen. Those same buddies, back in the day, were the ones who would chide me for passing on the attentions of the *dress blues groupies* who attended every Friday night parade and accompanied the Marines back to the barracks slopchute . . . and from there, on occasion, to the ladies' apartments. Not that I wasn't tempted, mind you. But my strict but loving and ethical upbringing had conditioned me away from the concept of sex without commitment, and from the concept of telling a girl you loved her just to get her into the sack. I know, I was a throwback; at least, that was what some of my barracks buddies said. But then I didn't have to deal with tears, recriminations, jealous boyfriends, and possible paternity suits either. I thought that made it a fair trade-off.

Most of the time, anyway.

Back to Sandrine, and the feelings that were percolating, at least in me, and maybe in her too. Our commitment, first and foremost, was to the mission. Beyond that, the deal was that I'd fly home and never see her, or Alter Earth, again. I'd go back to the airport, to Gus—who must be frantic by now wondering what had happened to me—and to . . . Jennifer? No, thankfully by the time I got back to my home, she'd have returned to hers.

That's just the way it was. I would fly home. And Sandrine would stay here. And that was that.

Or was it?

Damn, life was complicated. *But look on the bright side, Walker. You could die here, and all your problems would be solved.*

Considering what we'd been through already, and what still lay before us, dying seemed a real possibility.

The next day dawned bright and warm, but the atmosphere between Sandrine and me was still chilly. No, make that formal. Resigned. I wanted to make amends for my impulsive remark, but Sandrine's actions—coupled with her speaking to me only when necessary—indicated we should simply be on our way. It would be a long walk back to the plane.

In fact, it took two days. We walked along the edge of the forest, keeping the cliff in view to our right as reference. Also, thanks to the parachute, we carried an escape route should we be attacked once we reached higher ground. Around noon of the second day, we happened upon something that made me shiver in spite of the spring-like temperature: on the ground, beneath a platform built on the branches of a tree, lay a pile of putrefaction—all black fur, green flesh, and . . . white maggots. We were appalled by the sight and the smell, but had to appreciate the irony. For here was the dreaded spider, now serving as food for the flies.

Knowing where we were now, I guided Sandrine to the edge of the forest and saw the most welcome sight I could imagine: our blue-and-white Cessna Skylane, number N6124Q. It stood as we'd left it, like a faithful dog waiting for its master to return.

Sandrine exhaled audibly. "At last," she said.

"Yeah. Now run." And I did, as fast as my legs would propel me.

"What? Why?" she called as she followed. Then she turned her head to see six fennics charging us from where they'd been hiding.

We climbed aboard and slammed the doors just as the nearest fennic reached the passenger's door. The parachute made a lump between the seatback and my own back, but that was of no moment now. I pressed the throttle—and the plane leaped backwards, nearly slamming our faces into the glareshield. Damn, the prop was still in reverse.

On the plus side, the surprise maneuver nearly shook the rat man off. On the minus side, it didn't. One clawed pink hand held on to the wing strut. One foot was probably on the step mounted on the landing gear leg, with the other braced on the wing strut where it met the cabin. I pulled the prop control back, the prop pitch changed, and we began moving forward.

I taxied around to face the broadest expanse of flat land and dropped twenty degrees of flaps for better lift. Sandrine pressed her body against me, trying to put as much distance as possible between herself and the leering face on the other side of the Plexiglas. I glanced over. I wasn't surprised to see that it was Ulm. He had found the plane, and with his buddies had been staking it out from the concealment of the woods. We had stumbled into the clearing about a hundred yards closer to the plane than they had been.

I fed full throttle, and Two Four Quebec fairly leaped off the ground and headed toward the edge of the distant cliff. Ulm was still with us, his beady eyes wider than I'd ever seen them, his fur pressed back by the wind. I retracted the flaps and wobbled the wings in an attempt to shake him off, but his grip was tenacious. Both hands were gripping the wing strut now.

We made it to about a thousand feet above the ground, and I made a series of dives, climbs, and wing-wobbles to try to divest us of our burden. No such luck. I wished I had taken aerobatic training: a good hammerhead, where you climb vertically, stall, and pivot the plane to point the nose straight down, would surely have done the trick. Sandrine sat up straight and put her hand on my arm. "Aldenwalker. Do not shake him off," she said.

"What?"

"We can bring him with us to River's Reach, as a captive."

Of course. Force him to divulge whatever information the villagers need, and figure out a way to explain the plane later. "Okay," I said, facing her—and panicked. She hadn't pushed the door's locking lever down.

And at that moment, Ulm figured out how to open the door. His fingers found the latch, and he pulled.

He was strong, that much was sure. It would take almost superhuman strength to hold the door open against the slipstream, but then fennics aren't human. He held the door open with his right hand and snaked his left inside.

He linked his fingers to Sandrine's collar and began to pull. She screamed and pushed against him as hard as she could. It was no use. Ulm had forced the door full open and wedged his shoulder against the doorpost, giving him more leverage, and now his wrinkled ratty fingers locked onto Sandrine's throat. He was trying to pull her out of the plane. I couldn't begin to contemplate the rest of the scenario.

Sandrine's eyes were wide and her tongue bulging when I felt her left hand low on my leg and heard the sound of my knife's being freed from its sheath. A second later the fennic screamed, and I saw the knife, nearly hilt deep, in his forearm. Sandrine pulled the knife with all her strength toward his wrist, opening a wide gash below his fur. He snapped his jaws at her, but she backed away, and then he pulled his bloody arm and his body back outside the plane. Sandrine slammed the door shut, and I reached across her to ram down the locking lever. She dropped the knife to the floor and held her throat, her breath rasping and raw.

Outside, Ulm held on to the wing strut with his good hand as arterial blood spurted horizontally from his left arm. Would he live to see River's Reach? Would it be better if I waited until he weakened and tried again to shake him off?

It was Ulm himself who provided the answer, as we passed beyond the cliff's edge and flew over the desert barrens. He looked inside the plane, directly at me, and curled his lip in a feral snarl. Then, exerting supreme effort, he braced his feet on the strut and began to push himself toward the nose of the plane.

Oh no, not that. Just how vindictive could one person be? Then again, this wasn't a person.

"What is he doing?" Sandrine croaked through her distorted larynx.

"He's figured out what makes us go. And he's going to try to make us stop. I think by shoving his body, head first, into the propeller blades."

She cringed. "Could it work?"

"It very well might, damn it to hell."

The fennic reached forward with his good right hand to grasp the front of the nose, and threw his left arm across the cowling. Gouts of blood splattered against the windshield. He had to be weakening, but if he was, he showed no sign. Using his good right arm to pull, and his feet against the strut to push, he began to inch his body toward the prop.

On my own world, it wasn't unheard of for bird strikes to damage a propeller and clog the cooling vanes of an airplane's engine, resulting in a very bad day. As far as I knew, Two Four Quebec's engine didn't have cooling vanes anymore, but it did have a prop that was susceptible to chipping. If Ulm were to use his thick skull to chip a prop blade, it could throw the propeller seriously out of balance and stress it beyond its limits. Worst case, it would shake itself right off the prop shaft and spin merrily away, leaving the occupants of the plane anything but merry.

It was shake him off now or risk the plane's becoming a glider. Rocking the wings hadn't worked before; what else could—but then a light came on inside my own thick skull. I pulled the throttle all the way back, pushed the prop pitch into reverse, and fed throttle again.

The plane shook like it was coming apart. Relatively speaking, it was like we had stopped in midair. And just as your body is thrown forward in a car during sudden braking, Ulm's body was thrown forward too. He instinctively raised his hand to stop himself . . .

His fingers dissolved in a pink plume; then his hand; and then his wrist. I thanked the powers that be for reverse pitch, because the gobbets of fennic sprayed more forward than back. Ulm's frantic face was the last thing I saw as his body rolled off the cowling to plummet thousands upon thousands of feet to the desert floor. Part of me hoped he would still be alive when he hit.

Without enough airspeed to give the wings lift, Two Four Quebec shuddered and stalled. I pulled back the throttle, took the prop out of beta, and pitched the nose down to build up speed. Throttle forward, and we were flying again. I made a one-eighty and headed back to the higher land, flying over the fennics far below and northward in the general direction of River's Reach.

"We did it, Sandrine, we did it!" I reminded myself of the rooster who thought his crowing made the sun rise. But that was okay. Hey, we'd cheated death one more time.

Funny, Sandrine wasn't joining in the fun. In fact, she was whimpering. "No," she sobbed, and it took me a second to realize she was talking to herself. "No, no, no. You stupid, thoughtless . . ." And she leaned against me and actually bawled.

I put my right arm around her shoulder and stroked her cheek. "Hey, it's okay," I said. "We're on our way to River's Reach, and it's going to be fine. Trust me."

She looked up, and her eyes were red. "You do not understand," she said through her tears. "I never told Ander's mother that he is dead."

Chapter 32

In River's Reach, in the modest office of the village matriarch, Delphe dismissed her deputy with a perfunctory wave of her pudgy hand. Her administrative duties, such as they were, were minimal, but Delphe did all she could to make them seem more important than they were. Which made Delphe herself very important, by association.

Fortunately—for she would have been devastated had she known—she had failed to grasp that the council had appointed her to her exalted position by default; the job called for a figurehead, and most of the council, like most of the other villagers, preferred engaging themselves in more meaningful labors. Administratively speaking, River's Reach basically ran itself.

Delphe had been widowed some decades before, when her consort was killed heroically defending the village against the surprise fennic attack. When the vile creatures invaded, he led the futile but spirited defense with a fury no one could have known lurked within him. He was among the last to be cut down.

Delphe was not counted among the defenders—she had been heavily pregnant with Ander at the time.

The village patriarch—an ancient man barely able to swing a cudgel—had also died in the attack, and when it became apparent to the remaining council members that no one wanted to fill his office, they decided to award it to Delphe in posthumous (but tacit) tribute to her late consort.

Delphe's son Ander grew into a beautiful young man, both erudite and talented. As a child, his singing shamed the birds, and his insatiable thirst for knowledge was rewarded when as an adult he became one of the village's most revered teachers of children. Indeed, the only desire he seemed to have beyond teaching others' children was one day to teach children of his own. He wrote songs and poetry and excelled at the finer points of social interaction. All agreed, at least to Delphe's face, that her Ander was a treasure. (Behind her ever-broadening back, some raised their eyebrows and smirked. Him, they liked; his mother, they humored.)

Then *that woman Sandrine,* from the unnamed village to the east, arrived with her father—Oreste, she remembered his name was—for a visit. Except for their shared vivacity, Sandrine was almost the polar opposite of her son: physically adept, possessed of strength and endurance, and eager for sporting competition. She and Ander met at one of his public discourses, and afterward she presumed to make overtures to him. Well. To Delphe, this was not only improper, it was also shamefully scandalous.

My Ander, thought Delphe, *was too polite (or too weak-willed?) to resist the woman's obvious physical charms. Like an eager puppy, he tried to please her— by giving her freely of his knowledge while at the same time asking her to share hers with him. Unfortunately, most of the woman's knowledge was of the physical.*

Delphe could not countenance her Ander's sudden interest in the physical, for she considered physical prowess to be commonplace, and commonplaces were . . . simply common. His strengths were to be found in his mind; not in any foolish and ultimately fruitless ability to run a race or swim a stream or swing a sword.

Delphe secretly rejoiced when Sandrine and her father mounted their unicorns and returned to wherever it was they had come from. But her joy was short lived, for within a lune Sandrine returned, alone, and continued her relationship with Delphe's Ander as if they had never been apart.

After that visit, Delphe advised Ander that he should not see the eastern girl any more. After all, there were many available young women here in River's Reach who would be a marvelous match for him, and who had indeed spoken to her of their interest. But he replied that Sandrine was not only beautiful but also intelligent, sensitive, and caring. She may be somewhat impetuous, he acknowledged, but that only added to her charm. (*One woman's charm,* thought Delphe, *was another woman's vulgarity.*) And Sandrine had continued to return, and Ander had continued to see her, and Delphe had continued to fret while nibbling at her ever-present platter of munchables.

Then, after several days of private interaction from which Delphe had inexcusably been excluded, they pledged their lives and fortunes, each to the other. That was the last indignity. Sandrine and her Ander (not *her* Ander, not Delphe's Ander any longer) departed for the woman's village. Further, they would not allow Delphe to accompany them. The course was too long and too arduous for one of Delphe's years and lack of stamina, or so Sandrine contended, but she and Ander promised to return regularly, at least once a lune, to visit.

They did in fact keep their word, and each time Delphe noticed, with regret, that her Ander (she still could not think of him in any other way) had grown more fit, more muscular, more physically adept. Plus, he had allowed the hair on his face to grow. He looked older, more like the farmers who tended the fields between the walls of River's Reach and the river itself. He looked unabashedly . . . common.

She could not deny, though, that her Ander was happy. In spite of the fact that he was no closer to being a father than when he left—probably it was that Sandrine's fault—he said he was thrilled with the new children he taught and with all the new things he had yet to learn, whatever that could mean. And he began calling his mother *old lady,* as if it were a term of endearment rather than disrespect. It was enough to make her retreat more deeply into her matriarchal duties—as well as into her cornucopia of confections.

"It is as if they seek to vex me," she bemoaned to one of her women friends who came to visit nearly every day, coincidentally just in time for midday meal. "I even overheard my Ander during one visit—talking to that Sandrine—refer to me as . . . as a gossip."

"Do say," said her friend.

"This was unacceptable, and it hurt me deeply. I said nothing, of course. It seems a mother's lot is to suffer in silence."

"Children often disappoint their parents, Delphe," commiserated her friend. "Now, would you have any more of those delicious sweets?"

It was odd, now that Delphe thought of it, that when visitors from the villages to the west or east took consorts from River's Reach, our villagers without exception returned with them. None stayed here to live. Plus, any curious villagers who sought to follow them uninvited were somehow always discovered and sent back. This might be something to discuss at the next lunar meeting of the council. And had it not been more than two lunes, closer to three, in fact, since her Ander had last visited River's Reach? Time does pass quickly when one is so busy.

The door opened, and the deputy returned. "Visitors, Matriarch, approaching the gates," he said. Delphe pushed her considerable bulk off her chair and arranged her robes to meet the new guests. She walked outside and toward the village gate. Everyone from the eastern and western villages, she remembered, avowed that the trip to and from was long and hard, but strangely enough, when they arrived on their fancy unicorns they in fact looked not at all the worse for wear. Perhaps this would be another anomaly to discuss at council.

The gate opened, and this pair, at least from a distance, certainly did look much the worse for wear. Perhaps because they were on foot; had something happened to their mounts? One of them wore olive coveralls and the other yellow, but both were torn, dirty, and—could those brownish spots be dried blood? Their faces were dirty too, but even the dust of the road could not hide the fact that the man looked somewhat odd. His skin was pale, his hair was light, and his eyes looked strange—could they actually be blue?

The woman he was with, the one who slightly preceded him, was . . . no.

It was her Ander's consort. That Sandrine. With another man! Oh, this was beyond scandalous. And the woman appeared to be laughing, too!

Delphe stopped in her tracks. Let the hussy walk the rest of the distance to her. Let her explain this breach of decorum and good faith.

When the woman drew closer, Delphe realized that she was not laughing but crying. Her eyes were rimmed in red, and tears made tracks in the dirt on her face. A sudden fear gripped the matriarch, and it intensified when the woman stopped before her, trembled, and fell to one knee, her head bowed. No one ever bowed to another here.

The woman Sandrine looked up at the matriarch. "Delphe, mother of Ander," she sobbed, "your son is dead."

Chapter 33

That didn't go well, I thought, as the heavy-set woman crumpled to the ground like a deflated parachute and covered her face with a shawl. She looked like a trembling bundle of rags. Sandrine reached over to comfort her, but she was pushed away as a hysterical wail emerged from deep within those robes, robes that looked like they'd been bought at Omar's tent sale.

Others came running to us, some of whom recognized Sandrine. They barraged her with questions, while at the same time regarding me with more than a little curiosity. Sandrine stood up and wiped her face against her sleeve.

"My village was raided," she said to the others as she flashed me a look that cautioned me to silence. "By fennics. They killed many of us, including my mother and . . . and my dear consort Ander." The crowd cried out in anger, sympathy, and loss.

From the bundle of cloth at our feet came a wail: "And it did not take her long to find a replacement for my Ander." I quickly grew very uncomfortable.

"That is not true, Delphe. Please believe me." She scanned the others. "This is Aldenwalker, a visitor from another village far to the east of mine. We hid from the fennics and followed them."

"You followed them?" asked one of the older men.

Sandrine nodded. "Yes. And we discovered the purpose of their raid was not for food,"—she paused, to let that sink in—"but for slaves."

The woman Delphe stood slowly. Sandrine tried to help her up, but the woman brushed her hand away. "What does this have to do with us?"

"What it has to do with you, Matriarch, is that our own captives joined others already enslaved in the fennics' caves. And I would assume," Sandrine added, "that the ancestors of those captives originally came from here in River's Reach."

More cries came from the crowd. Older people looked at each other and spoke names, names I judged were those of their friends and relatives captured some thirty-odd years ago. Then we heard cries for revenge, cries for freeing the slaves and bringing them home.

"We can tell you where they are and how to get there," Sandrine concluded.

With their minds stunned by this news, no one, thankfully, asked us where our unicorns were. The plane happened to be waiting in a clearing behind a hill a mile or so from the village.

I understood why Sandrine didn't want to mention the gorgons. The villagers simply didn't have the need to know—at least not for now. The need-to-know concept I knew well, from my Marine Corps duty in Washington. One crisis was enough for them; the other one belonged to us alone. Again, for now.

The matriarch begrudgingly gave Sandrine and me rooms—separate rooms—in her home. We washed our coveralls as well as our bodies—separately, again—and later in the evening sneaked out for a stroll, successfully avoiding curious citizens whose questions we couldn't or wouldn't answer. The episode with Ulm had resulted in a thawing between us, and our comfort level with each other had almost returned to, well, to comfort. Our walk took us along the village wall. On top of the wall we saw a walkway, patrolled by guards, now more alert than ever for a possible new fennic raid. The council—having debriefed us—was at that moment meeting to form a strategy to destroy the fennics and retrieve their human prisoners. Meanwhile, villagers milled about the council chamber, buzzing among themselves, anxious for information and some hint of resolution.

After the confusion and sadness of the afternoon, we were happy just to be by ourselves.

"Delphe does not trust me," said Sandrine. "She thinks I corrupted her son, when in fact I liberated him. She smothered him with her affections and affectations."

"Maybe she simply didn't want her son to meet the same fate as his father."

She thought it over. "That is logical, Aldenwalker. He and I used to joke that she wanted to keep him in baby's napkins until he slipped into old age and became like a baby again. Baby naps from birth to death."

"I'm sorry you had to lose him."

"And I am sorry you had to lose your love."

We stopped and faced each other. Our eyes, I thought, were communicating something words found difficult. Remembering what I'd stupidly uttered earlier, when we were huddled beneath the parachute to shelter us from the rain, I decided to keep my big mouth shut. Sandrine parted her lips as if she were about to say something, but she must've thought better of it. She turned and continued to walk. Whatever she had intended to say—or do—the moment was lost.

"Delphe is a bitter woman," she said. "I have not provided any sweetness for her today."

"What is she to the town, anyway? People seem to defer to her, and you called her Matriarch."

"The title is largely honorary. It is voted on by the council to pay tribute to someone who . . . these are Ander's words, not mine . . . has no real use but who needs to feel useful."

"Huh. In other words, she needs to play with the bigness of her littleness."

"Excuse me? What was that? The bigness?"

"It's a line from a poem I remember reading, memorizing in fact. Does it fit?"

Sandrine cocked her head. "It fits perfectly. Do you like poetry, Aldenwalker?"

"Some," I admitted. "Does that surprise you?"

She looked as if she were going to say something, but again thought better of it. She lowered her face, but I caught the faintest of smiles.

I said, "Wait. Academic question coming. How can you have poetry when your language has no figures of speech? It's an oxymoron, like the sound of silence, or negative good, or . . . or honest politicians."

"Believe it or not, we manage to manage without them."

"And Oreste: I heard some of your folks call him Patriarch. Is he considered useless?"

"No. My father is respected for who he is, not for what. His honorific is deserved."

"That I can believe. He's thoughtful, intelligent, and carries himself with dignity. I like your old man, I really do." That brought her smile from faint to full.

On the wall above us, a guard walked his post, his figure limned by the waning gibbous moon over his head. As I watched, the moon suddenly faded out, to be replaced by what looked like a hole in the sky. Suddenly my legs felt like they'd been plunged into ice water.

"A portal!" I whispered. "Look!"

Sandrine gripped my hand hard as we watched the portal descend upon the hapless sentry. It stopped at his waist. He looked about frantically and appeared to scream—we heard nothing—as the portal winked out. Most, but not all, of him went with it. The lower half of his body dropped to the elevated walkway, and seconds later two dark streams spilled over the edge and puddled at our feet.

"It has begun," said Sandrine, anguish in her voice. "We are too late."

Chapter 34

We had neither time nor inclination to explain what had happened to the villagers. We hurried through the nearby gate and closed it behind us. The moon was back where it belonged, and River's Reach was quiet. When it came time to rotate shifts, the guard, or what was left of him, would be discovered, and we didn't want to be around when he was found. Some of the townsfolk already looked upon me with suspicion, thanks to my somewhat alien appearance, and I wondered if that would be enough for them to associate me with the sentry's death.

"Maybe it's not too late," I said as we hiked toward the hill that hid the plane. "Evidently, the gorgons still haven't learned to fine tune their bridge. They'll need to practice some more."

"I think they believe they are ready now. Maybe they severed him from his legs to taunt the people, put them in a state of fear."

"You mean like the state I'm in now."

Sandrine looked at me frankly. "And I."

We made it to the plane and climbed inside. It was still dark, which meant it was the middle of the day for the gorgons. "Let's try to catch some sleep," I suggested, and we did. Try, that is. And mostly we failed.

Eventually the sky began to lighten, and after our morning ablutions—happily, the river was nearby—we re-boarded Two Four Quebec, fastened our seat harnesses, and prepared to leave. The parachute was stowed on the floor of the luggage compartment behind the rear seats, and our swords rested on the seats themselves. We would put those on after we landed.

Drawing a deep breath, Sandrine took the explosive from the glove box in the instrument panel and put it in a pocket of her coveralls. The remote detonator, its switch caged to prevent accidental activation, she put in another.

We faced each other. This was it, perhaps the last time either of us would have the luxury of a quiet moment together. "Before we go," I began, "I need to apologize for my remark—"

She placed two fingers against my lips and said, "Shhh. There is no need. And no need to cloud our thoughts with emotion. Certainly not now. Maybe . . . maybe later." She gave me a slight smile and lowered her hand. "The longer we delay . . ."

I let out the breath I didn't know I was holding. She was right. I looked around to clear the area and fed in the throttle. After a brief roll we were airborne, retracing our route to the south before bearing west when we passed the edge of the plateau that bordered the barrens. Thirty minutes into the flight, with the morning sun taking the chill off the cabin, we saw a silver ribbon to the north. It led to the waterfall where we'd met Moby Worm and I'd gotten this distinguished-looking crease across my nose. I gave Sandrine the yoke and told her to ease us down below the mountains rising to the west. "Follow the river below the falls to the sea and turn right," I said. She still tended to overcorrect a bit, but she was developing some real skill at the controls. And she did enjoy the flying . . . almost as much as I enjoyed watching her fly.

Once over the ocean, we looked back at the mountains that rose steeply from its depths. One of those peaks looked like it had been cut flat and leveled off. That had to be our landing strip. We were in the mountain shadows now, and the chill was back. "Make a circle to the left and climb," I directed. We spiraled up until we were level with the plateau. The rising sun hit our eyes, making us squint in the glare. To the left, the black face of the seaside keep loomed skyward.

No traffic pattern applied here; I took the controls, flew straight in, squeaked the tires on the level rock surface, and braked to a stop. "Good landing," Sandrine observed. Everyone's a critic, it seems. Or had she just been trying to lighten my mood?

We taxied past two openings with sliding metal doors near the far end of the mountain wall, and I turned the plane around to park it between them. One of them, Sandrine told me, had to lead to the storage bay where the casks of Power would almost certainly be kept.

I shut the engine down, and we got out and strapped on our swords. One set of doors was partially open, enough for us to slip inside without making noise. When we did, we were instantly hit by the eye-watering, nose-burning stench of ammonia. "Guano," I whispered. Sandrine nodded, and we inched forward, trying to breathe without inhaling.

We passed a room whose door was ajar and peered inside. Now I knew what hell looked like. The only thing missing was a sign that read, *Abandon All Hope, Ye Who Enter Here.*

The room looked like a morgue, and maybe it had been back in the day. But today it was . . . well, it was still very much a morgue. Except that the body we saw wasn't dead. But it wasn't alive either. One drawer had been pulled out from the wall, and two of the most hideous creatures I'd ever seen were hunched over the body of the man strapped to it. The slab on which he lay had been fitted with a pair of tiny metal stands, and to each stand was attached an IV bag. An elevated one contained a clear liquid; the other, which hung just below body level, contained a dark red medium we recognized instantly. The clear liquid fed into the victim's left arm; the red drained from his right. He made no move; his eyes were closed in deep lethargy—or in coma.

One of the monsters, smaller than I but far differently proportioned with short legs and long brown arms, removed the full bag from the victim's right side and replaced it with an empty one. The other slid the body back into the wall. The one holding the bag caught a red drop on her finger (it was definitely a female, judging by her flaccid, pendulous dugs) and licked it clean with a purple tongue, before putting the bag into what looked like a refrigerator. Her companion yawned loudly—those teeth! And the two of them left by another door.

For the moment, Sandrine and I forgot about the stench. These poor people, these human victims, gave new meaning to the term *living dead*. They were zombies—senseless, stupefied, existing in some obscene state of suspended animation. How many drawers were there? How many victims occupied them?

Reason told me they couldn't be saved when we blew up the keep; that even if we could get them out, their brains were probably vegetated anyway; that their sudden extinction would be a blessing. I hoped Sandrine felt the same way; I could see her fingering the detonator through her pocket flap.

She nodded to her right, and we continued past a few closed doors until we reached a flight of stairs. "We have entered through the wrong door," Sandrine said. "The storage bay must be through the other one."

"I don't think you've come through the wrong door at all. I'd say you've made an excellent choice of doors."

The voice wasn't mine. It was high-pitched, sibilant, and came from a mouth a good foot higher than my own. Sandrine and I spun around and stopped as if we'd been turned to stone. Indeed, if anything could turn a man to stone, it was the sight of this.

It was a gorgon.

Chapter 35

"I am Ibliss," the thing hissed, "and I welcome you to my keep. We have so few guests these days—so few willing ones, anyway." He must have thought this joke most clever, judging by his wheezes.

He held his arms out to the side, his wings fanned out behind him like Dracula's cape. His hands were tipped with claws the size of a bear's, but no one would mistake this thing for Gentle Ben. His chest was massive, like a fifty-five-gallon drum mounted sideways above a wasp-like waist. And like the females, his legs were short. The bottoms of his wings attached to the small of his back. His body was covered with matted brown fur, and his face was wide, with narrow-set red eyes and a thin muzzle that housed flaring nostrils, black lips, and a frightful set of stiletto teeth. When he opened his maw, drool spilled down his chin.

"You must be the offworlder," he said, once more catching me completely off-guard.

Sandrine grabbed the detonator from her pocket and looked at me. "Go ahead," I said, but before she could uncage it the gorgon swatted it from her hand. *How could he have been so fast?* I wondered. I barely saw him move.

"What else might you have hidden on your person, female?" His voice dripped contempt.

A claw ripped down Sandrine's other pocket, and the bomb fell out.

"I'll get that," said a familiar voice from behind me. I turned around, and suddenly everything became clear.

Scud.

Sandrine looked from the gorgon to the fennic and then to me. Fear and rage fought for dominance on her face. I guessed mine looked the same. I lunged for him, my hands reaching for his throat, but another hand gripped my own neck instead, so tightly I felt like my eyes would pop. Ibliss had, in fact, grabbed both Sandrine and me, holding us back so that Scud could pick up the explosive. The fennic disarmed us next, including the sheath knife at my calf, and with a series of self-satisfied chuckles walked up the stairs to a catwalk. Ibliss indicated we were to follow him.

At the head of the stairs, we turned into a room filled with the same kinds of machinery I'd seen in Oreste's keep. Ibliss swung the door closed. At least the ammonia smell hadn't infiltrated here. A viewscreen, like a giant flat-screen television, dominated one wall. It was a match for the one in Oreste's keep.

The gorgon shuffled over to a bank of controls and instruments while Scud barred the door, his own sword out and his narrow black lips drawn back. "A shame about Ulm," he said. "But I think he was making plans to challenge me anyway, so there's no great loss. He joins Orr and my sentry Lud at the base of the cliff, food for the vultures. The others, the ones you did not send to their deaths, reported back and told me of your airship."

"And the rest is history," I snarled.

"Exactly. Did you notice the mortuarium when you came in? We just provided a new batch of slaves for it. And when I told Ibliss's couriers my news, they flew me here to report to him directly. And to wait for your arrival." The rat-thing smirked. "It didn't take long. I knew it wouldn't, especially after our little demonstration last night with the guard."

"How convenient."

A hiss interrupted us. "Watch, offworlder. I think I've nearly mastered this device. Forget the fennic and look at what the master of the gorgons can do." Neither the rat nor the bat seemed to take Sandrine's presence as particularly noteworthy. A cultural thing,

I guessed, if such a word could by any stretch of the imagination be applied.

The screen came to life. On it I saw a seascape from some unimaginable time and place. Nightmare creatures, some with tentacles, others with eyes on stalks, all with mouths or other orifices filled with row upon row of jagged teeth, did battle above the waves and disappeared beneath them. *Lord,* I thought, *don't send us there.*

But Ibliss had no intention of sending us anywhere. "I have discovered other worlds," he said. "But this is the one I want you to see, offworlder." The picture flickered and disappeared as he made further adjustments. I wanted to cry at what he pulled up next.

The buildings were unmistakable. It was my world, my country, the city where for my last two years in the Marines I'd served my country. Ibliss jockeyed a joystick and gave us a tour. There was the Capitol; there, the Lincoln and Jefferson Memorials, the Washington Monument, and nearby the White House. Sandrine looked at me, and I nodded grimly. "Mine."

The gorgon moved a slider, and like the zoom lens on a camera, we closed in on a slum-ridden section of the city. Closer and closer we got, until I could see individual people walking on the sidewalks, all unaware of the menace that hovered invisibly above them. It was dusk, and the streets had already been abandoned to those whose natural element was the dark.

We saw a woman, elderly, behind a walker, hurrying home to her tenement. In an alley perpendicular to her path hunched a man, poised, waiting. A knife in his hand glinted in the streetlamp's light.

"Watch," repeated the gorgon. The screen showed a quick zoom in—Ibliss punched a button—and a quick zoom back. The man was gone. The elderly woman shuffled past the alley, forever unaware of how close she'd come to bleeding her life out on the cold pavement of the inner city.

And in a blaze of cognition, I understood how utterly vulnerable my own world was to this terrorist from another dimension. Further, how the task of saving my world had suddenly devolved onto just two people. Two people who now stood hopeless and helpless to thwart the gorgons' plans.

A scream came from behind us, a human scream, causing Sandrine and me to spin about. Between Scud and us stood the mugger. He wore an army surplus jacket over camouflage trousers. That was all we could take in before we saw that those trousers terminated at the knees. The lower halves of his legs were actually locked into the floor of the lab.

Legs and stone, impossibly occupying the same space at the same time. Molecules intermixing, competing, the organic yielding to and becoming part of the inorganic.

I had never heard such anguished cries in my life, had never dreamed such agony could come from a human throat. Through his pain, the mugger was able to see Sandrine and me—and then the gorgon behind us. The shrieks became falsetto, like a pig's in a slaughterhouse, and Ibliss calmly walked over, extended a talon, and silenced the scream.

"I see I still need to practice my precision," he said. He tilted the man's head back farther than nature had ever intended, wrapped his jaws around his neck, and drew on it as if it were a straw. The man's frantic flailing stopped, and eventually the gorgon stood upright, his muzzle dripping gore. "A bedtime snack," he said, and laughed.

Scud joined him in this rollicking good time as Sandrine and I backed away, horrified. The mugger's head was hanging behind him, like some kid's cowboy hat on a string.

"Cousin," said Ibliss to the fennic, "I trust you can keep watch over our guests until this evening's entertainment. I am already overdue for my rest."

"It will be my pleasure," said Scud as he flicked the mugger's knife toward himself with the tip of his sword. "Can I tell them just what that entertainment will be?"

"Of course. Anticipation is half the fun." The door opened, closed, and we were alone with Scud—and the other abomination stuck in the floor.

"Against the far wall," growled the fennic, motioning with his sword. "Unless you would care to break your fast with me?" We said nothing. "No? I thought not." Then he took his sword to the dead man's body.

Sandrine and I sat in the corner, huddled together. I clasped her hand, and she pulled my arm around her shoulder. We couldn't watch Scud eat—listening to him eat was bad enough—and when he was done, we tried to ignore his description of what he was going to do to us tonight after the gorgons woke up.

Last night, in River's Reach, Sandrine had been right. We were too late. If only I hadn't stopped to pick some strawberries after we'd been forced down by the storm: I wouldn't have been captured by the arachnids, and later by the fennics; Sandrine and I wouldn't have had to trek through the desert to find a way back to the plane; my nose wouldn't have been smashed by the bloodworm; we wouldn't have had to hike back to the plane; we wouldn't have had to detour to River's Reach; all (except the nose thing) were time devourers. Without that *if only,* our mission would well be over by now, most likely for the better, for the gorgons wouldn't have been expecting us.

And now it was clear that all these delays combined spelled doom—not only for the human population of this world, but also for the human population of my own.

Chapter 36

As he gleefully reminded us many times during his first Earth-human feast, Scud intended to slice and dice me, slowly and oh-so-painfully, and then, in a magnanimous display of his generosity, turn Sandrine over to the gorgons for draining. When he had finished his grisly meal, he herded us at sword's point to a windowless room containing a door to a lavatory. The room looked untouched from when people had lived here, except that it was devoid of furniture. Maybe a bed was offensive to gorgons. Maybe they slept upside down, hanging from their feet, and didn't even know what a bed was for. Who knew? All we knew was that we were to spend our last day in a square, poorly lit room: bare gray walls and a black stone floor. When Scud closed the door, we heard something being dragged against it. After we'd waited a few minutes, we tried pushing it open, but it wouldn't budge.

Most of the time we sat with our backs to the wall. I put my arm around Sandrine, and she leaned into me. There were times we dozed, more from stress than exhaustion. Our stomachs rumbled every now and then, reminding us that we hadn't eaten since last night. A pall hung over us, and I found myself counting the seconds and minutes and begrudging each and every one that led us closer to our deaths.

When the door opened, Sandrine was asleep, curled up on the floor with her head in my lap. She opened her eyes and sat up alongside me. We didn't stand. Our eyes were blank, our faces expressionless. We had adopted the mindset of the condemned.

"Get up," said Scud. "It's already well into the night. You kept Ibliss up beyond his bedtime this morning, and he overslept. He woke up with an appetite." The fennic snarled, and I could see tiny scraps of mugger flesh still stuck between his pointed teeth. "Plus, he informed me after this evening's festivities are completed I've got to supply him with more slaves. Which doesn't seem fair, does it?" I couldn't stand the sneer on his rat face. He was having too much fun.

"Makes sense," I grunted. "You took the place of one of the slaves Ibliss sent his boys for. Last thing he wanted was more *dead weight*, isn't that right, ratso fatso?" Man, I said to myself, what am I doing here? Well, I'd be dead soon anyway, might as well get some licks in first.

Scud grunted back. "I wouldn't try to insult me, offworlder. I can kill you swiftly or slowly, it's my choice."

I shot a glance at Sandrine, then back to Scud. "Ibliss lets you have a choice? Why, you must be very grateful to your master. I'll bet if he wore boots, you'd be keeping them clean with your tongue. In fact, if you weren't such a pussy, Scud, you'd give me my sword and make it a fair fight."

The fennic seemed about to say something, then stopped. "You know," he said slowly, as if thinking took more effort than he was used to, "that might be a good idea. I'll be back." He closed the door and barred it.

"Everybody wants to be Ahh-nold," I muttered to myself.

"You said he beat you when you fenced before," Sandrine said. "Let me fight him."

"Because you're better, you mean."

"Yes. Because I am. And because it would surprise them, catch them off guard. After all, females do not seem to garner much respect from either the fennics or the gorgons."

Okay, Walker, she's right, I thought. *But chivalry demands . . . no, chivalry is peculiar to my world, my culture. Here on Alter Earth, there's no such thing as* the weaker sex. Vive la difference *doesn't go beyond plumbing. Still, how could I bring myself . . .*

"Sandrine, you're right. You should fight him—but even if you win . . . we lose. We're outnumbered. We can't save ourselves, and we can't save your world—or mine. We've failed either way. We're done. They win."

"Then why did you bother to challenge Scud?"

"We have a word on my world. It's *pissed.*"

She lowered her eyes, then looked into mine. "From your tone, I think I understand."

"If I have to go out, I want to go out swinging."

The barrier was dragged away, and the door opened again. "It's agreed," announced Scud. "We'll meet the gorgons in the storage bay. There's more room there for us . . . to play."

The fennic prodded us to the cage of a freight elevator—not unusual, as this had once been a human habitation—and pushed a button. We descended to the ground level, where six gorgons, Ibliss and five others, waited for us in the storage bay we'd hoped we were entering earlier today—or was it yesterday by now?

The gorgons were smarter than I'd given credit for. Thanks to Scud, they had known we were coming and made sure the storage bay door was closed and the other partially open, so we would try that one first and walk right into Ibliss's trap. So simple, so effective. And we were so stupid to fall for it.

Scud lifted the cage door and, like a private with delusions of being a general, marched us to the center of the room. Near the door to the outside, I counted eight small casks, each the size of the tubs you see sitting in the freezers in ice cream shops.

"Are they what I think they are?" I asked Sandrine.

"Yes. Six of them are ours." She added, bitterly, "Were ours."

"Welcome," greeted Ibliss, arms wide and grinning, as if he'd just stepped out of a Bela Lugosi movie. "I've invited some friends, as you can see. Every performer needs an audience, I'm told." The gorgons formed a circle around us, with Scud and me in the center and Sandrine close to the periphery. Not too close, though, as these gorgons might be thirsty.

"Are you going to give me a sword, there, Scud, or are we going to go at it hand to hand? Before you answer, I think it only proper to advise you that my hands are registered with the authorities as deadly weapons."

Despite herself, Sandrine snickered, and when the nearest gorgon looked at her she covered it with a cough. She looked at me and shook her head. Her eyes told me she was as devoid of hope as I, but there was something in her resigned smile that spoke volumes about her courage. I saw something else in that smile, too, and it bolstered my own courage: an emotion that I'd thought I wouldn't be seeing again, at least in this lifetime. I smiled back at her, which irritated Scud that my attention wasn't on him. After all, this was his show.

"You're trying to get me angry," he said, his black lip curling in a sneer. "Make me careless. Do you really think I'm that stupid, offworlder?"

"I really couldn't say how stupid you are. But I do suspect you couldn't count your balls and come up with the same number twice."

Sandrine pressed her hand to her mouth.

As I'd noted, I was dead anyway, so what the hell? If I couldn't cut him down physically, I'd settle for verbally. Ibliss and his buddies were laughing, and it gave me a perverse pleasure to know it was at Scud's expense.

"I was thinking of killing you reasonably quickly," said the fennic; an obvious lie. "But now I think it'll be agonizingly slow—with a tiny nick here, a little slice there, a small amputation here and there." He pointed his sword at my crotch. *Gulp. Not so funny anymore.* But I was determined to keep up the façade. If I had any chance of bettering him, it could only be by making him furious enough to make him careless.

So I yawned and looked at the gorgons. "Did one of you guys break wind, or was that just Scud talking? Hard to tell from here."

More laughter from the peanut gallery.

Scud rushed up and grabbed me by the collar, twisting it. "I am going to enjoy killing you." He brought us eyeball-to-eyeball.

"Whew! You going to do it with your breath? How do you do that, Scud: fart through your mouth?"

He roared and threw me to the floor, then drew his sword.

"Right," I said, from my sprawled-out position. "Kill an unarmed man. I'd expect nothing less from you, Scud."

Ibliss interrupted. "Give him a sword, Scud. And I hope yours is sharper than your wit."

Scud was about to growl something back, but he thought better of it when he looked into the *ampair*'s yellow, vertically-slit eyes and fang-studded grin. He grabbed the sword he'd taken from me and slid it across the floor. I got to my feet and bent down to pick up the blade. This was it, Custer's last stand. Where'd all those Injuns come from?

"Aldenwalker!" The shout came from Sandrine, and I looked up to see Scud charging me, sword poised for a chop. I dropped to my knees at the last second and rolled against his shins. The sword swung down, but missed as the fennic tripped over me and fell flat on his barrel-shaped belly.

I jumped to my feet and grabbed my sword. *Let me run him through,* I prayed, *before he can get up.* But he was too fast, and we squared off, facing each other, swords clashing. We pushed each other away, and then I found myself on the offensive. Scud backed off for a second, stood flat-footed, and shook his head once, as if to clear it. Then he returned my attack, slash for slash.

The gorgons laughed at our flailing. They sounded like a stable full of whinnying horses. Sandrine leaned forward, probably looking for an opening where she might join the fray. But then a taloned hand gripped her shoulder and forced her upright again.

I saw this during another brief interlude while my opponent backed off and shook his head. Then he was on me again with renewed vigor.

He forced me against a wall, both of us breathing hard. He was by far the more experienced swordsman, but for some reason he wasn't pressing his advantage. Maybe my strategy had had an effect? Well, I could try again. Our faces were inches away when I forced a grin and said, "Had enough?"

The fennic's beady eyes narrowed and he pushed himself off. I ducked just in time to avoid a swinging blow as he stepped back.

But then he got me.

It was on his backswing, which I hadn't expected. I had sprung from the wall, intending to press his retreat. But he stopped short, went into a squat, and sliced. I saw a line drawn through the chest of my jumpsuit, ending at the zipper. An electric thrill accompanied the slice, then a sting, then the blood. His sword was double-edged. I'd not noticed.

I heard Sandrine shout, and that seemed to energize me. I leaped at Scud, surprising him and making him back off. The circle of gorgons expanded and contracted around us as we continued to thrust and parry, first one and then the other having the upper hand.

Then he got me again.

My shoulder this time, the left one. His sword arced and ground against bone. I yelped, I'm not ashamed to admit, and both hands went numb. My right nearly dropped my sword, but I forced myself to hold tight when I saw Scud's leer.

I brought up my sword, too late to ward off another cut, this time on my right thigh. Scud drew a red line down the left side of my chest next. I glanced over and saw Sandrine struggling to free herself from the gorgon holding her, weeping in fury. Then I looked back to Scud. He was smiling. "Now it begins," he gloated. "Death by a thousand cuts."

I could barely breathe, could barely hold the sword up anymore. And when Scud made his next cut, and his next, all I could do was watch dumbly as one more stripe of blood turned my yellow jumpsuit red. I had lost the ability to feel pain. I had almost lost the will to breathe.

Scud paused for a breather of his own. He looked at Sandrine, now mute with horror, looked at the gorgons for their signs of approval, then turned back to look at me. Another tiny jab, another delicate slice, none of them deep, none of them to a vital area. I felt like Julius Caesar on the ides of March. *Et tu, Brute?* When would the fennic deliver the coup de grace?

Barely able to stand, I lowered the sword, held it at my side . . . gave up. I knew it was over. *Lord, let me die with dignity.*

Then the strangest thing happened.

Chapter 37

I actually felt myself leave my body. Rise, incorporeal, into the air. There was no more pain, no more exhaustion, just an overwhelming and abiding sense of peace. I had done my best, and now I could claim my rest, my reward for a job well-attempted, if not well-completed. For a life lived honorably, if not particularly heroically.

Around and about me I seemed to sense another presence. This was nothing physical, for the physical was but a memory now, like a dandelion seed blown away by the breeze. But I had clearly been joined by another, a presence I found somehow comforting and familiar as I looked down upon the scene below me and saw:

The storeroom.

The freight elevator.

The eight casks of Power.

The six gorgons, standing in a circle.

Scud, breathing heavily, savoring his victory, his sword point resting on the floor, wondering where to cut me next.

My body, standing there, helpless, waiting for death and accepting it.

And Sandrine, behind Scud, head bowed, the hand of the gorgon standing behind her released now from her shoulder as his attention grew fixed on the fennic.

The other, the presence with me, directed my attention toward Sandrine. To see into her future. She would be led to a draining table, where her life's blood would be drawn to feed the gorgons; for as long as she continued to live, she would also be dead. The thought was unbearable. *No!* I cried for her.

The presence with me or within me spoke. It was not with an audible voice; still, it was one I could not help but recognize. It was a voice which once vowed *'til death do us part* and whose last words to me were *I do.*

Do not lose her, the voice said. *You must not lose her, too.*

Then it was gone, and with blinding speed I was sucked back into a world of hurt. The fennic chief stood before me, little big man, ready to lift his sword for one more cut.

A red veil fell across my eyes, and a last burst of adrenaline shot through me as I roared and hurled my sword at Scud.

He ducked.

"I learned," he crowed, but his satisfaction was cut short by a sound behind him. Sandrine had ducked too when she saw the sword flying over Scud's head, but the gorgon behind her hadn't had the foresight to do the same. The sword skewered his neck like a shish kabob. He grasped at his throat, gurgled, and fell. Sandrine took a step to the side. The others stared, unmoving.

Then Ibliss laughed.

And the others joined in. Including Scud. There was one gorgon that wouldn't condescend to him any more. Scud had remembered his own lesson from my time in the fennics' cave. And now his teacher-cum-opponent was unarmed. All attention returned to the fennic and me.

"What will you do now, offworlder, hmm? You have no weapon. Unless you count those *deadly weapons* at the ends of your arms." He was seized by an amusing thought. "Do you know? I think I'll cut off those deadly weapons. One finger at a time. And make you watch me suck the meat off each one before I lop off the next. What do you think of that?"

All eyes were on Scud. No one but me seemed to notice the movement behind him.

"I think you should think again," I said—and before he could respond there came a silver slash from behind. Following a solid *chunk*, his head veritably leaped from his shoulders and dropped into my hands. I looked at the head fennic's head and saw his amazed expression. His eyes blinked at me, and his jaw opened and closed, then went still. His body stood upright for a second more, as if it didn't know it was dead, and then fell forward, the stump of neck spouting blood. In the fennic's place stood Sandrine, my Amazon, my angel, her black eyes blazing. No one had noticed her take the sword from the fallen gorgon's neck. No one had bothered to pay attention to her. She was a female, after all. She was of no consequence to either fennics or gorgons.

Another lesson learned. One alienated this angel at one's own risk.

In a single motion, I tossed Scud's head at the shocked Ibliss and picked up the fennic's sword. The *ampairs* were taken by surprise, and their talons, with their short range, proved no match for long blades of sharp, swinging steel. We hacked them apart, and they went down without a sound.

Sandrine and I looked at each other, at the carnage we had created. And we fell into each other's arms, exhausted.

"She told me not to lose you, too," I panted, looking deep into Sandrine's eyes.

We stared at each other for a brief moment. She might have been holding me up.

"Let's get out of here," I said, "before someone figures out something's wrong."

"Aldenwalker," she reminded me. "The Power."

"Yes! Hurry and get it loaded!"

We slid the doorway open to see the golden light of dawn push above the horizon. The plane stood ready. The Plexiglas windshield picked up the sun and reflected it into our eyes. The gorgons, the rest of them, would be going to sleep now. We might make it after all. If only I could stop bleeding . . .

We picked up the casks of Power, one at a time, and ran them to the plane. I tipped the front seat-backs forward, and we tossed them into the back. With two casks remaining, I chanced one last look at the six grotesque bodies and the spreading pools of blood around them. Sandrine picked up one cask and I picked up the other and noticed something.

"Wait. The lid's loose on this one." I lifted it to find it filled to the brim with tiny granules of multicolored iridescence. This was what we had come to retrieve. This was what would allow the keep to continue as it had. This was what would send me home. A treasure that would put King Solomon's to shame.

I held the lid up with my right hand and casually reached my left down to sift once through this all-purpose pixie dust—

And choked back a scream.

My eyes fixated on my fingers.

My fingers, that were already one knuckle deep in the Power.

One finger still wearing my wedding ring.

My *gold* wedding ring!

Chapter 38

Sandrine saw my shock. "What? Come, we must hurry!"

"Do you see what I almost did?" I stammered as I gingerly withdrew my fingers, being extra-special careful not to bring some grains of Power up with them.

She noticed my ring and said dismissively, "Aldenwalker, the Power does not react with silver, only gold."

"Uh huh. May I assume you've never heard of *white* gold?"

Now it was her turn to shake. "Put that lid on, quick! Use your other hand!"

"No kidding!" But I hesitated. "Wait."

"Wait? Are you mad?"

"Do you remember we have another job to do?"

I pulled the ring off—and looked for the last time at the engraving on the inside: *For Alden, forever.* I put it in my pocket, then carried the cask to the freight elevator. I pressed the button that sent it back up and found I could still reach the metal grate on the bottom of the cage. Cutting off a length of lace from my boot, I looped it through my ring and tied it to the bottom of the cage. "Thank you, Lynda," I whispered. "I won't lose this one."

Then I scattered a handful of Power on the floor directly beneath the ring.

"Okay," I said. "Now let's get out of here." I clamped the lid down on the cask, and we ran outside. Into the back it went with the others. We flipped the seatbacks to their normal position and climbed inside. "Make sure your door is locked this time," I remarked, and Sandrine slammed the lever down with authority. "We're getting out of here, rikki-tik."

We didn't bother fastening the harnesses. I just pushed in the throttle.

And as I did, we saw gorgons, dozens of gorgons, emerge from the keep.

The Skylane flew into the air, just ahead of the vampiric air force. The plane built up speed as we cleared the keep and flew over the ocean. Through the rear window, Sandrine watched our pursuers finally give up the chase and turn back. We lowered the nose to level flight and turned south, to retrace our way to the barrens and from there to the keep.

"Something wrong, Aldenwalker?"

"Nothing, I guess. Weight and balance seem to be off. I'll just adjust the trim here." I turned the trim wheel up, the effect of which was to angle the nose down, and soon we were back to straight and level flight. "The casks must add more weight than I thought." Then I thought of something—two some-things, actually—I should have known and cursed myself.

"What is it?"

"Sandrine, why would gorgons need to use elevators? They fly."

She thought for a second. "Oh."

"One other thing."

"What?"

"Something was wrong back there. In the storage bay."

"Wrong?"

"Did you count the bodies?"

"No."

"I did. There were six. But one of them was Scud. That left five gorgons."

"But there were six, were there not?"

"Alive, there were six. Dead, there were five."

"That means—"

"It does, indeed," hissed a high-pitched voice from behind us.

At that moment, my bowels turned to jelly.

Sandrine looked back and screamed.

"Very interesting," said Ibliss from his perch in the back seat. He had somehow squeezed into the luggage compartment before we'd begun loading the casks of Power. Some of them had gone into the back seat, some had fallen over and onto him as he squatted there.

After announcing himself, he had climbed over the seatback, moved casks aside to accommodate his bulk, and sat in the center of the seat behind us. In our haste to get away, we hadn't bothered to look, we hadn't even thought to check.

If we had, we could have skewered him with our swords before he had a chance to strike. How many more screwups could I make and still come out of this alive?

"I wondered how your little toy worked, wondered what it would be like to fly with someone else's wings instead of my own. Rather pleasant," he hissed. "Certainly not tiring."

Our swords lay on the floor in back, where Sandrine couldn't reach them. Scud had taken my sheath knife in the keep, and where it was now was anyone's guess. We had no weapons available to us at all.

Except for the plane.

I'd never considered being a *kamikaze* before, but if it came to that . . . and then it hit me.

Ibliss was as much our prisoner as we were his! I turned my head and looked at him.

"You smile," said the gorgon. "Why?"

"I'll never tell."

Sandrine stared at me as if I'd finally snapped.

"Look, Sandrine," I said and nodded out the window, pointedly ignoring Ibliss. We were nearing *our* meadow, the vast expanse that bordered the waterfall.

Sandrine looked down and smiled wistfully. "It was a good place," she said. Evidently, my verbal *faux pas* down there was forgiven, if not fully forgotten.

"I have seen enough," said our stowaway. "Turn around and return to my keep. My friends will be waiting."

"How many *friends* do you have there, Ibliss?" I asked.

"Oh, very many. While you were cutting down my closest, I sneaked out and told the others to allow you to escape, then pretend to give chase when you flew away. Just to keep you alert, mind you. And to keep you distracted from what was riding in the space behind the rear seat. It worked, didn't it?" He wheezed another laugh.

"To a point," I agreed. "But only to a point. See, my new best friend, we're not turning back."

"What?" asked Ibliss.

"What?" asked Sandrine.

"We're not turning back. Period. Is there some part of *We're not turning back* you don't understand?" I shrugged my shoulders, exaggeratedly. "Okay, big guy, tell you what. If you want to go back, you're free to leave whenever you want. But . . . oh, damn, there are no doors in the back of the plane. And the luggage door opens only from the outside, and it's too tiny for you to fit through anyway. Sorry, pal. Looks like you're trapped in here with us."

"You're not funny."

"Not trying to be, pal. So, why don't you just sit back, relax, and enjoy the ride? Sorry, but we can't offer in-flight movies this trip. It won't be that long."

Ibliss hissed. "Turn around."

"Make me."

Sandrine had turned sideways in her seat. Her back was against the door, and she looked open-mouthed at both of us. She'd never played chess, but she recognized a stalemate when she saw one.

Except that I had one more gambit left.

"Watch this!" I called back and pushed hard on the yoke. The nose pitched forward and—whoops!— we roller-coastered down an invisible track. The gorgon was lifted from his seat, as were we. But his gourd hit the headliner and ours didn't.

Now I pulled back on the yoke, and the G force pushed us down into our seats. The nearly weightless casks of Power were flying around, knocking against him, keeping him annoyed, if nothing else. Next came a steep bank to the left, followed by one to the right, into a descending spiral. Full power next, and up we went, only to do the vomit comet routine once again.

I felt hands around my throat, hands tipped with black claws. "Good, choke me to death, you dumb bastard. See where that gets you. Like, smashed against that cliff down there. Remember, dummy, you can't get out of here. You'll die along with us."

"You wouldn't kill yourselves!"

"We would!" shouted Sandrine, as she tried without success to pry the gorgon's fingers from my throat. "Two lives are nothing measured against millions. I would gladly die to save them! Dive, Aldenwalker, dive!"

The fingers loosened their grip, let go, and I felt my windpipe begin to seek its original shape. Meanwhile, a retching sound erupted from the back seat.

"Aldenwalker, he just puked!"

"Is that what I smell? Yuck! And I forgot the bags. You airsick, back there?"

"No, it is more than that," she said. "I think he is dying."

Chapter 39

"I'm going to put down in the meadow," I said. "I think it's flat enough."

"I hope it is. That smell is enough to make me puke, too."

"Is Ibliss really dead?"

"I think so. His eyes are open, and he does not appear to be breathing."

"You don't die from airsickness. At least, not on my—wait. Comes the dawn."

Sandrine looked back at me. She got it, too. "It would explain why Scud seemed ill when he fought you."

"Despite the fact he was making a pin cushion out of me? Thank you so much for the morale boost." She touched my sleeve, looked at one of my many cuts, and smiled. None of them was as deep as they felt, although some would benefit from a Betsy Ross treatment. Thankfully, there was the first aid kit inside the glove box. There's no such thing as being too prepared.

"That monster from your world was going to kill a defenseless old woman," Sandrine said, and I acknowledged that my world probably had at least as many monsters as this one—but they were harder to spot, because they looked just like us. "Instead," she continued, "the microbes from his world killed two monsters on this one."

"Someone they ate disagreed with them," I observed and began setting up our approach.

The first thing we did upon landing was to open the doors wide to let the air circulate and get the stink out. I lugged Ibliss's body out onto the grass, intending to take it to the waterfall and give it the famous float test, but Sandrine stopped me. With first aid kit in hand, she led me to the water's edge and told me to get my jumpsuit off and slip into the icy stream.

"Oh, man! It stings! I don't know which is worse, the cuts or the water."

"This is no time to pretend to be a baby," Sandrine chided.

"But it feels so good to be treated like one," I said, adding, "Mommy."

Sandrine doffed her own overalls then and slid in beside me. Beneath them she wore a one-piece under-garment that I decided was most unflattering—until her body reacted to the cold, that is.

"Stop staring."

"It's a guy thing."

"You're lucky I don't have my sword."

"Oh yeah? You're lucky—hey! You used a contrac-tion."

"I did not."

"You used two, in fact."

"I do not crush my words together. It is undigni-fied."

"All right, have it your way."

"Stop your silly grinning. Now hold still and let me check your wounds."

After we decided I would live, Sandrine dressed the worst of my wounds; then we scrubbed our coveralls on rocks and hung them over a tree limb. Only then did we drag the gorgon's body to the waterfall. I'd have to invent some new adjectives if I were ever asked to describe just how ugly he was. His namesake Medusa was Miss America by comparison. It took both of us to haul his carcass to the falls, and once there, I grate-fully gave his body a nudge. It eased over the edge, bounced off one rock after another , and splashed into the pool below. It bobbed up and down for a few min-utes before suddenly disappearing beneath the sur-face. I didn't see what had grabbed him; nor did I even remotely want to.

"I'm so hungry—" I began, and Sandrine finished the sentence for me.

"Your stomach thinks your throat has been cut. It was funny . . . once." Ouch. But her tone and her smile were free of any hint of judgment. She spotted a batch of wild strawberries nearby and brought them to me. "Strawberries," I said. "The beginning of all our problems. If I hadn't noticed them in the woods after the storm had passed and just gone back to the plane—"

Sandrine pressed two fingers to my lips. "The strawberries are also the reason you found the fennics and their slaves, and the reason one day soon those slaves will be free."

I considered this as I ate a berry. Its juices nearly spilled from my mouth. "You know, by rights these berries should be tasteless. They're too big. On my world, it's the smaller berries that are the sweetest."

Sandrine lay back on the grass. "What do you mean, on your world, Aldenwalker?" Her tone was different now, with a playful lilt that I found irresistible.

I lay on my side next to her, elbow against the ground, my head propped on my hand. I looked at Sandrine lying there, her eyes closed, her lips barely parted. "You know, I don't think I can say that anymore." Then I leaned down and kissed her.

"Mmm," she said when our lips parted company. She looked through half-lidded eyes into mine and murmured, "Tell me about your poetry, Aldenwalker," she breathed, "what you call figures of speech."

I decided I liked where this was going. This wasn't a delaying tactic on Sandrine's part; it was a prolonging of anticipation for what we both silently acknowledged was happening. And to accommodate her, I would begin by touching Sandrine's most sensitive erogenous zone: her mind.

"Okay then."

"As in acknowledged? Or okay as in all is well?"

"Maybe both. We'll start with what we call metaphors." I defined the term, but she asked, through barely-moving lips, for an example. "Hmm. Let me think a bit . . . okay, I've got one. But I'll paraphrase, with apologies to Robert Herrick."

"A poet on your—on the other world?"

"That's correct. Are you ready?"

"Yes."

I closed my eyes. "Whenas in silks my Sandrine goes, then, then, methinks how sweetly flows the liquefaction of her clothes."

She thought for a minute. "What a lovely word, *liquefaction.* It means the light ripples off the fabric, as if it were water?"

"You've got it."

"I like it. But, Aldenwalker, how would you know? You have never seen me in reflective fabric."

"No, but I'd like to one day."

"Mmm. More examples, please."

I leaned a little closer, my lips inches above her own. "Shall I compare thee to a summer's day?"

She reached up and drew my lips to hers, then covered my face with kisses while I played my lips over her nose, cheeks, eyes, and ears before moving to her chin and neck and farther south.

After a time that might have been minutes or as long as an hour, we lay beside each other on the grass. Sandrine lay in my embrace, her head resting on my chest. She turned her face up to look into mine and sighed one word: "Ohhhhhh . . . kayyyy."

I slipped two fingers beneath her chin, locking onto her gaze, and gave her my pledge. She sidled up so that her face was directly above mine. "I accept your pledge," she whispered, her dark eyes bright, her breath soft and sweet on my face, "and I offer you mine."

As day became evening and the sun went down, we made love again, this time more confidently, more slowly and playfully, accompanied by giggling, teasing, outright laughter, and Sandrine's unrestrained shout at our moment of mutual climax: "Sacred excrement!"

Then the world blew up.

Chapter 40

It was as if a hydrogen bomb, minus the mushroom cloud, had exploded to the west. As soon as I saw it I knew the reason, something I hadn't noticed or paid attention to upon our arrival at the gorgons' lair. The females we saw had no wings. They would have every reason to use the freight elevator if they needed to get down into the storage bay from the floor above. And for their lack of wings, at this very moment a mountain was being reduced to rubble. The mountain . . . and everything and everyone inside. Including those poor, comatose, human wretches suffering in half-life. At least they would have no idea of their fate, and perhaps from some other realm they would bless us for setting them free.

Sandrine and I sat up and turned our eyes from the blast, which outshone the afternoon sun by many magnitudes. Then I pushed her to the ground and told her in no uncertain terms to roll onto her belly and plug up her ears. I lay on top of her. Chivalry may be a non-issue on this world, but old habits are hard to break.

Our meadow lay some fifty miles from the keep. Doing some quick math—something pilots learn to do, it's a survival skill—I estimated that in about ten or eleven seconds the sound would reach us. And reach us it did.

With the deafening, nearly concussive, roar came the wind. Gale force. Hurricane force. F-5 tornado force. By the time it passed, our ears were ringing and stinging, and our bodies were covered with leaves, sticks, ash which had fortunately cooled during their flight, plus other assorted debris; thankfully, no gorgon body parts.

When the shock wave passed and all was quiet again, we stood up and brushed each other off, and that led to—well, never mind. But know that good things come in threes.

I hugged Sandrine to me and whispered in her ear, "Did the earth move for you, too?"

"I think," she whispered, hugging me back, "that you might have used a little less Power."

We stayed in the meadow another day, ostensibly to scrub gorgon goo from the plane and to allow my fennic-inflicted wounds more time to heal, but who were we kidding? We just wanted the time to be with each other: to talk, to play, to celebrate each other's bodies and commune with each other's souls. Sound corny? Too bad. If it sounds that way to you, you're obviously jealous.

True, with another day's delay, Oreste and the others would be more than fearful for our safety, but we figured they'd understand. And if they didn't, well, the Russians have a saying: *Tufshitsky*.

First stop was a brief one at River's Reach, where we entered on foot, with the Skylane hidden behind the same hill as before. Everyone was still anxious, having seen the flash of light and heard the resulting explosion. We explained to Sandrine's former mother-in-law along with the town council that their sentry's death had been a one-time-only horror: that we'd seen a gorgon—yes, they were real—swoop down and sever his upper body with a sword and then carry it away. They listened intently as we described our trek to follow it to its lair, hoping to kill it. But after only a day's travel, we felt the earth begin to shake. Suddenly the sky lit up, as what must have been a volcano erupted. We barely found shelter, and anything closer—as the gorgon most certainly was—had no chance at survival. And if there had been more gorgons, they too would have been vaporized in the blast or killed by the concussion.

When we were finished with our story, we promised to return before long for the purpose of training them for their upcoming attack upon the fennics. Rescuing the human slaves from their bondage had become an obsession with the townsfolk, but without any military expertise they would be virtually helpless. My memories of my favorite drill instructor would provide me some background relative to discipline, and Sandrine would ensure their prowess with weaponry.

Delphe looked at us with unspoken acknowledgment. There might have been gratitude in her face; then again, it might have simply been resignation. Finally, we headed out for the plane's hiding place and flew back to the keep.

A hero's welcome awaited us. After we told our story, Pandora said the next day she'd assemble her crew to replace the Cessna's engine. I told her thanks, but no thanks. She frowned at me, then turned to Oreste; Oreste frowned at Sandrine; and Sandrine smiled sweetly at both of them. Her father understood, and as a pledge present he offered me a surprise.

It seemed that back in the day, the ancient scientists of Alter Earth had discovered a way not only to create a portal between worlds but also to fold the time continuum to project into the past. They called it the temporal bridge. To access it required a large amount of Power, but evidently he figured his new son-in-law had earned it.

"You're telling me you can send me back to the time you snatched me away?" He nodded, and I looked into Sandrine's face. "I accept the offer. I have some loose ends to tie up, and some friends who will be worrying about me. One condition, though: you bring me back here when I'm done." Sandrine's smile lit her face, and I kissed her.

"Say no more, young man."

"Thanks . . . old man."

He shook my hand.

I was back in the silent Cessna, alone, flying the reciprocal of the course I'd flown more than a month before. Right on time, I saw a hole in the sky, the same portal through which I'd flown in an earlier, unsuspecting life from an earlier, endangered but unaware Earth.

And there I was, in the other Skylane, heading right at this one.

I flew through the portal and swerved to the right to avoid a mid-air. At the same time, the earlier Skylane swerved as well, its panicked pilot nearly dirtying his tidy whiteys. (I remembered.) A few seconds later, I wiggled my wings in salute, and laughed at the thought of the furious gesture my earlier self had returned.

A thought struck me. What if for some reason I hadn't avoided the mid-air? What if the two of us had collided and exploded, somewhere over the Virginia piedmont? I pondered that paradox all the way back to the airport.

Chapter 41

Before I told them anything, I lifted the cowling's inspection port and showed Gus and Jennifer what was inside; rather, what wasn't inside. That made the rest of the story easier to tell and easier for them to accept. The telling would take well into the night.

First, though, I had Gus call our attorney and arrange immediately for a document giving him full power of attorney over all my earthly possessions, with the exception of Two Four Quebec. With POA, he was my custodian of record. He could at any time transfer title to the airport and everything on it to himself. He could move out of his flat and move into my family home. He could sell everything, take the money, and retire to a tropical island with a *wahine* on his arm and a rum punch in his free hand. For all intents, everything I wasn't taking back with me was his. My gift was something he couldn't dismiss with his usual bluster, and for a second there I thought he might even cry.

Second, I packed the luggage compartment of the plane and piled up the back seat and floor with a stack of my clothes and personal effects, including photos of my parents taken when the damage that would kill them was still hidden inside their bodies and behind their smiles. I picked up my favorite photo of Lynda, wearing her jumpsuit, perched prettily on the step of the jump plane. I studied it for a bit, and then—after a delicate kiss and a murmured word of thanks—decided to leave it behind.

Finally, I told my story into a tape recorder as the three of us sat around the kitchen table. Jennifer said she'd cook a spectacular farewell meal for me, and we ended up dining on overdone burgers and French fries that had come from the freezer. No vegetables. Still, she was actually proud of her meal. Gus and I humored her and told her it was great.

Afterward, Jennifer announced she'd stay behind to do the dishes: "I'm proud to be a full-service caterer." Gus shook his head, took the tape cassettes, and told me he'd see me in the morning.

The door slammed, and Jennifer rushed into my arms.

"Whoa!" I said. "Jennifer?"

"This is our last chance, Alden, can't you see that?"

"Jennifer, didn't you hear a word of what I said? I'm spoken for. Happily and evermore spoken for."

"Yeah, like on another world. Alden, think about it: like, duh, who's going to know?"

"Like, duh, me, Jennifer. I can't do it. Thank you; thank you a lot, but no."

Her eyes filled up, but I couldn't tell if it was from anger or hurt; maybe it was both. "Then you won't see me tomorrow when you leave. I couldn't stand to say goodbye to you, not like this, not like forever." She kissed me, hard. "So long, Alden. Have a good life."

The front door slammed, her car door slammed, and I stood by the window watching her taillights fade into the night. Then I walked through every room, inventorying it—not for physical possessions, but for memories. Tonight would mark the last time I would sleep here, alone, in the house I'd grown up in, and the thought—instead of inducing melancholia—made me want to sing.

True to her word, Jennifer was not around the next day when Gus came to say goodbye. He met me outside the ops building, gave me the power of attorney form to sign, mumbled some profanity-laced words of endearment, hugged me (for the first time ever), and then gave me a shove toward the plane. "Sure I can't convince you to take you-know-who with you, Walker? Get her out of my thinning hair for good?"

"What would you tell her father?"

"I'd make up something. Hell, he might not even realize she's gone until it's time to pawn her off on me again next summer."

"Well, sorry, Gunny, but that's something you're going to have to deal with yourself."

He shook his head. "She was gone this morning when I woke up. Told me last night she'd be heading to Ocean City today. You'd think she'd want to say goodbye."

"She said goodbye last night."

"Didn't take her long. She pulled up just as I was turning my key in the door."

"Good thing, huh? If she stayed longer, you'd think I took advantage of her after you left. Gave her one for the road, so to speak. And you'd be standing here today with your Colt forty-five pointed at me."

"Walker, if that were to go down, she'd be the one takin' advantage of you. Course, that don't mean I wouldn't track you down with my full arsenal anyway."

We were still laughing as we arrived at the plane. Another hug—the man was still a bear—and I climbed inside, closed and latched the door, and flipped open the side window. "Clear prop!" I called, closed the window, and taxied the silent Skylane to the runway.

The sky was the deepest blue I'd seen in many a summer's day. The inversion that usually plagued summertime airport operations had lifted, and I took off with a feeling of contentment deeper than any I'd ever known before.

A little more than an hour later I saw it—the portal, the hole in the sky, the bridge between worlds—on time and in place, just as Oreste had promised. Nothing was flying out of it this time, thank goodness. I looked down and to the side and took my last glance at the world of my birth, then looked ahead into my new world, the world I would no longer think of as Alter Earth.

I was going home.

Epilogue

Gunnery Sergeant August Bellows, USMC, retired, watched Two Four Quebec fly into the western sky, watched it grow smaller until he could no longer see it. A lump came into his throat, and he forced it down with a scowl, daring it to return.

A brace of skydivers had chuted up and were walking toward the jump plane. A good day for jumping—no haze, no wind, no problems. A good day for flying, for the same reasons. A good day, in fact, for a lot of things, not least of which was planning his move from the one-bedroom apartment he rented (he slept on a lumpy couch during Jennifer's visits) to the stately Walker family farmhouse near the entrance to Walker Field.

Not a good day to say goodbye.

Gus walked from the tie-down area back to the ops building. As he passed the parking lot, he spied Jennifer's car parked between the two airport vans. She must've changed her mind about spending the day at the beach, he thought. Probably changed her mind about not saying goodbye to Walker. Well, you're too late, girl. Tough titty, Tootsie, he's already gone.

He glanced again at the car. It didn't seem fair that he should drive a ten-year-old Honda while his sandbagging niece got a brand new BMW from her rich-assin daddy for her eighteenth birthday. *Some day you'll get a reality check, kid,* he thought, *and then you'll see what it's like to live in a world that—surprise, Jennifer!—doesn't owe you a living.* Gus had railed at his brother, loudly and often, for years. "Don't you see, you're handicapping your kid by making her life too easy?" But did bro, with his wildly lucrative business ventures and his string of trophy wives, listen? Hell, no. He just broke out his checkbook. Daddy could always tell whenever Jennifer was going to ask him for something: her lips moved. And he still didn't get it.

Her father gave her everything she ever wanted . . . but none of what she desperately needed.

Oh well, not my problem, Gus thought as he walked into the office and gave Joy the bookkeeper his cordially gruff good morning.

"An envelope here addressed to you, Gus," she said. "Found it on my desk when I came in."

Gus took the envelope—something was lumpy inside it—and went into his office. What was this about?

He sat at his desk and opened the envelope. The keys to Jennifer's Bimmer tumbled out first, followed by a photograph—Jennifer in her high school graduation robe. Okay, he thought. Very nice. But . . .

Then he pulled out the note and read it.

All at once, it was not a good day at all; in fact, it was a very bad day.

"By the Commandant's balls," he muttered. If he had been standing, he would have fallen over. Since he'd given up the stogies, Gus was healthy as a horse, but he thought for a moment he might be having a coronary. Hell, considering what he'd just said to Walker—but it was a *joke*, damn it—he deserved it. He shook his head as he re-read the note, especially the last paragraph, written in her loopy penmanship with the little circles over the *I*s:

Make sure to tell Daddy I love him. Oh, and tell No. 4 too, I guess, just to be polite. But it's really you I love most of all, Unca Gus. Always have; always will. Thanks for caring. Jennifer (the twerp).

Gus looked westward out his office window, and for a long minute he simply stared. He placed the note on his desk alongside the keys and the photograph, then he picked it up and read it again.

"Jesus H. Christ," he said, his voice imploring. "Just how in the seven hells am I gonna explain *this* to my brother?"

About the Author

Stephen M. DeBock is a Marine Corps veteran who served in the Presidential Honor Guard during the Eisenhower and Kennedy administrations. A private pilot and former liveaboard boater, his non-fiction has appeared in *American Heritage, AOPA Pilot Online,* and *Living Aboard* magazines. He wrote the text for a coffee-table book titled *The Art of H. Hargrove* and writes the artist's quarterly fan newsletter.

His novel, *The Pentacle Pendant,* in which a contemporary werewolf becomes a one-woman star chamber, is currently available in hard cover, eBook, and trade paperback. Two of his e-publications from Gypsy Shadow have been listed among the top horror stories of their respective years.

Stephen and his wife Joy live in Hershey, Pennsylvania.

FACEBOOK
https://www.facebook.com/pages/Stephen-M-DeBock/29503417388799